# THE BODY POLITIC

## VICTOR GOLD & LYNNE CHENEY

ST. MARTIN'S PRESS ★ NEW YORK

Portions of this book previously appeared in *The Washingtonian* magazine.

**Design by Judith Stagnitto.**

Library of Congress Cataloging-in-Publication Data

Gold, Victor.
    The body politic / Victor Gold and Lynne Cheney.
      p.   cm.
    ISBN 0-312-02171-2
    I. Cheney, Lynne V. II. Title.
PS3557.0353B64    1988
813'.54—dc19          88-12016

First Edition
10 9 8 7 6 5 4 3 2 1

To Hannibal Hamlin,
the first Republican Vice President
(dumped by Abe Lincoln, 1864)

For the great majority of mankind is satisfied with appearances, as though they were realities, and is often even more influenced by the things that seem than by those that are.

—**Machiavelli,** *Discourses on the First Ten Books of Titus Livius*

Whenever there is a vacancy in the office of the Vice President, the President shall nominate a Vice President who shall take office upon confirmation by a majority vote of both Houses of Congress.

—**Section 2,** the Twenty-fifth Amendment to the Constitution of the United States


"When I go, I want it to be the way it was with FDR and Kennedy—people saying for the rest of their lives, 'I remember exactly what I was doing when I heard the news.' "

—**Stewart Bulloch Vandercleve** in a moment of hubris, circa his third campaign for the U.S. Presidency

SEGMENT ONE

## THE VICE PRESIDENT'S TOWNHOUSE

### (MIDNIGHT)

★ To get there you follow Route 50 going northeast into the city, and it is a good highway but under repair. Or was under repair, the night I got the call. I made the turnoff into Rosslyn, racing across Key Bridge, not slowing until I hit the crunch on M Street, thick with Mercedes and Volvos, the yin and yang of Georgetown traffic; then hung a left at the second traffic light, moving into the dark corridors of residential Washington at its best and at its worst; best because this was the high-rent townhouse district inhabited by upscale Washingtonians who couldn't abide either the bourgeois suburbs or condo life at the Watergate; worst because at that hour odds were that one out of every five houses I passed was being burglarized.

Not, however, the house at 5614 Dumbarton Place where the red brick Federal had round-the-clock protection—two armed guards parked in front, three more posted in the rear courtyard. Only three kinds of VIPs could afford that kind of muscle by the 1990s: Japanese investors; white-powder entrepreneurs; and top-of-the-line U.S. government officials.

I parked the car half a block down and began sprinting—not the shrewdest way to approach a Secret Service detail at 12:10 A.M. There came, in my instant before peril, the sound of car doors opening and slamming. Two shadowy hulks pincered me as I neared the wrought-iron fence.

"Hold it, sucker, right there."

A forearm shiver braced my clavicle, spinning me into the grasp of a second agent. The blinding glare of a pocket flashlight pierced the dark.

"Frank Lee . . . what *you* doin' here?"

Albert Shelby, tight end, New York Jets, 1981–85.

"My mistake, Al," I croaked. "Should've worn my staff pin."

Shelby doused the light and signaled the second agent to release his grip. "Right," he said, "but that don't answer my question."

"Got a call," I replied, still sucking wind.

Shelby's massive head moved up and down in the darkness. I could feel, if not see, his sneer. The truth was that the Number Two man on the Vice President's protective detail didn't especially like me. Nothing personal. It was just that Shelby hated the news media, and as the VP's press secretary I was, by his lights, little more than an enemy collaborator.

"A call," he repeated tonelessly, tumblers obviously clicking inside his head: A call to Lee at midnight? Weird. But he's senior staff and has access. If the Man really wants him at this hour, fine; if not, it's his wagon, not mine.

"Right," said Shelby, having run through his options. "But next time, get your joggin' in before midnight." He straightened my coat collar. "You okay, Lee?" he asked, simulating compassion.

"Just fine," I lied. "No harm done."

Waving his partner back to the car, Shelby swung open the

fence gate, then led me across a brick walkway to the door, which he proceeded to unlock but not open.

"Your move," he grunted. I turned the knob, then entered a semidark foyer, its watered silk walls illuminated only by light from the top of the stairwell. As the latch snapped to, there came the same unmistakable telegenic voice I'd heard over the phone a half hour before.

"Frank?"

Romana Clay, network news superstar, no doubt about it.

"Frank?"

"Coming."

Under normal working conditions, I am a hyperkinetic stair climber, taking two steps at a time; but on this occasion a dull ache, running from my third vertebra to my sacrum, discouraged haste. That and a sure professional instinct that foretold unwanted news at the top of the staircase, some fitting climax to an extraordinarily shitty day at the Office of the Vice President.

## THE VICE PRESIDENT'S SCHEDULE

### MAY 12

| | |
|---|---|
| 7:30 A.M. | Depart residence for Executive Office Building |
| 7:45 A.M. | Arrive EOB |
| 7:50 A.M. | Leave EOB for White House |
| 8:00 A.M. | Breakfast meeting with the President |
| 9:00 A.M. | Return to EOB |

*"Dumped!"*

It had begun on a note of towering outrage, shortly after nine that morning. The Vice President first raised then lowered a clenched fist, as if jerking the chain on an antique toilet in one of his overseas vacation villas. *"Dumped!"* he repeated. "Just like that!"

The fist came down in a perfect ninety-degree arc, scattering state papers and lesser memoranda across the EOB office. A solid gold pen holder shaped like an oil well, a gift from the Crown Prince of Kuwait in happier times, teetered on the edge of the cluttered mahogany desk, then fell to the floor. An intriguing blue-black Rorschach slowly took shape on the Persian rug, joining indelible stains that evidenced previous high-level staff meetings.

McCluskey and I, knowing the folly of interrupting our patron midtantrum, received the news in silence. The VP chief of staff and I sat side by side on the blue camelback sofa beneath a portrait of the Vice President's favorite forebear, Theodore Roosevelt, and waited for the storm to pass. When it did (9:16 A.M.), the Vice President sagged into his chair, his face assuming an expression as dour as that of his least favorite forebear, John Adams, whose portrait hung on the wall across the room. McCluskey made a rattling sound as if to say something, then thought better of it. That left it for me to take the plunge.

"Any options?"

*"Options?"* The Vice President stirred, rising to remove his coat (Blades, Savile Row) and strip off his tie (Sulka). "Lots of options," he said, launching both coat and tie in the direction of a nearby Louis XVI chair. "I can, one, voluntarily withdraw from the ticket now; or two, get my ass booted off at the convention next month."

He slumped into his swivel. I pursed my lips. McCluskey grunted. The intercom buzzed. Bristling, the Vice President hoisted the receiver to remind his secretary, Ms. Littlepaugh, that he'd ordered a hold on all incoming calls, including those of his wife, ex-wife, brothers, even the executor of his blind trust. He listened a moment, muttered, "Tell General Mize I'll talk to him when I'm damn well ready," then slammed down the receiver.

Mize. That would be General Maximilian Mize, Director of the Federal Bureau of Investigation, though I had no idea why he'd be calling. I looked at McCluskey for a hint. He shrugged, shaking his head. There was a moment of uneasy quiet, broken only by the rush of heavy Vice Presidential breathing, until the intercom buzzed again. This time, an explosion: "MS. LITTLE-PAUGH," he began, "I TOLD YOU POSITIVELY NO CALLS. . . ." Then: "Oh, *him*. . . . You're right. I'll have to take it."

A gravid pause while, if Washington experience was any guide, two secretaries played the status game of each not putting her boss on the line until the other's had gone on first. Then, with no hint of whose eyeball had finally blinked, the Vice President, his voice exuding cool patrician cordiality, was saying: "Hello, Regis? Yes, I understand perfectly. The President's in a helluva spot. . . . Absolutely. No hard feelings. As a matter of fact, my staff and I are going over the scenario this very minute. We'll get back to you."

He dropped the phone into its cradle. "Strong, the bastard," he rasped. "Afraid I didn't get the message the first time around."

McCluskey cleared his throat. This time he spoke up. "Was Strong at the breakfast?" he asked, an obtuse question typical of McCluskey, who must have been the only person in Washington who hadn't noticed that, except for thirty minutes at the House rostrum delivering his annual State of the Union speech, the President was never seen without his chief of staff within whispering distance.

The Vice President nodded, yes. He leaned back and closed his eyes. Then: "Lee, you know what I need?"

Since he'd framed the question in the rhetorical imperative, I waited to find out who or what he wanted fetched. Eyes still closed, he pointed toward a hidden wet bar in the alcove adjoining the office.

"A stiff pop," he said. "The usual."

Again McCluskey found his voice. "Before noon?" he exclaimed. "Far be it from me, Mr. Vice President, but you have an eleven o'clock appointment with Dr. Kissinger."

"Shred it," snapped the Vice President. "Also my luncheon speech at the Federal City Club."

"Cancel the *speech?*" McCluskey gasped. "But the White House Communications Office specifically asked—"

"I said, shred it," repeated the Vice President. "Shred *all* my appointments for the day, the month, the year. Frank, I said I needed—"

"Right." I headed toward the alcove, pausing only to retrieve his haberdashery and fold it neatly across the Louis XVI. At the bar, I opened the louvered floor-level cabinet and withdrew a miniature bottle of Chivas Regal, then remembered his specific instructions and took out a second.

"YOU WANT THE TRUTH?" the Vice President bellowed from the office.

"WHENEVER POSSIBLE," I bellowed back, dropping ice cubes into a heavy crystal glass bearing the blue-and-gold Vice Presidential crest.

"I GIVE HIM CREDIT," he shouted. "AT LEAST THIS TIME HE HAD THE DECENCY TO HANDLE THE JOB HIMSELF. RE-MEMBER LEFFINGWELL?"

Ah, Leffingwell, our esteemed Secretary of State, once removed. He was called out of his pew at St. John's Church one Sunday morning by a White House military flunky who advised him that the locks were being changed on his office and his personal belongings had been carted away. Where, the flunky wanted to know, did the ex-Secretary want them shipped?

"BUT HE LIKED LEFFINGWELL," I shouted back, pouring the contents of both miniatures over the cubes. I added water, stirred, then stepped back into the office, picking my way across the paper litter. "In your case," I said, handing him his drink, "he *wanted* to do the job himself."

"You're right," he grimaced; then, more to himself than us: "I should never have taken this job," he said. "The man hates my guts and always has."

It was a fairly accurate assessment of the President's feelings toward his Vice President. Also a warning that we were about to enter into the second phase of Vice Presidential distemper, generally characterized by equal dollops of sardonic self-pity and smoldering resentment. This in turn would be followed by a third phase—an air of aristocratic insouciance that told the world: *What the hell do I care? I can buy 'em all out!*

Unnerved, McCluskey instinctively went to his knees and began moving about, snatching up memoranda.

"What's the timing?" I asked.

"Oh, he was generous," replied the Vice President, rattling the ice in his glass. "I asked if he wanted me to announce I wouldn't be a candidate for renomination immediately, this afternoon, and he said, no hurry, tomorrow morning would be time enough."

"A Saturday morning news conference?"

"To hit Sunday's papers." He inhaled the Scotch in two quick gulps, studied the Vice Presidential crest on the empty glass, and pitched it into a wastepaper basket. "He flies to Madison right after church to hustle the governor's endorsement. That's what it's all about. He wants a liberal on the ticket to pick up votes in Wisconsin. If I'm not a candidate for renomination, he can use the Vice Presidency for bait. He'll need all the lib votes he can get to beat Stanton in Tuesday's primary."

McCluskey was on his feet now, a mass of documents clutched to his ample midsection and a puzzled look on his face. The Vice President's chief of staff was a reasonably competent office manager, but as a political operator Martin Aloysius McCluskey was *sui generis* in Washington: a naïve, teetotaling, humorless Boston Irish Republican. It was a distinction which, for reasons not clear to me, endeared him to Bully Vandercleve, the ultimate WASP.

"Have I missed something?" McCluskey asked. "I mean, Mr. Vice President, I understand why you're being, as you put it, dumped—Senator Stanton challenging the President for the nomination, the Wisconsin primary—"

"Yes, Mac, I just went through all that," the Vice President said indulgently. "What is it you missed?"

"That business about the President—uh—hating your guts."

"Oh, that," said the Vice President with the patience of an elder dealing with a backward child. "Well, Mac, it has to do with my being Stewart Bulloch Vandercleve and the President's having had to wait tables to put himself through some second-rate law school down South. With my wife's being a tennis champion at Stanford, while the First Lady was taking a mail-order charm course. With my being born with class and his having absolutely no class at all. Get the picture?"

McCluskey's eyes widened. "But that doesn't make sense," he said. "If the man hates your guts, why would he pick you to be his Vice President?

Bully Vandercleve laughed; his sardonic, self-pitying laugh. "Can you think," he said, "of a *better* reason?"

He leaned forward, retrieved his glass from the wastepaper basket, and held it up. "Hit me again, Frank," he said. "Shorter on the extras this time around." I returned to the bar, poured another stiff one—two miniatures, no ice, no water—and brought it to him. He took a deep swallow, coughed, and gave an imperial wave of his free hand, a signal that our presence was no longer needed or desired. "Get to work," he said. "Shred those appointments and hack out a statement for tomorrow morning's news conference." He drained the glass. "My swan song to this whole miserable business."

McCluskey and I got up to leave.

"What the hell do I care?" we heard him mutter as we headed for the door. "I can buy 'em *all* out."

**MEMORANDUM**

## OFFICE OF THE VICE PRESIDENT
### WASHINGTON

DRAFT—VICE PRESIDENT'S WITHDRAWAL
STATEMENT

   I have a brief statement, after which I'll take questions.

After a long period of soul-searching and discussions with members of my family, I have decided not to offer my name to the Republican National Convention for renomination to the office of Vice President.

~~I have consulted with the Presid~~

The reasons for my decision relate to my personal desire, after nearly three decades of public service to devote ~~to dedicate my full energies to give more time to~~

BULLSHITBULLSHITBULLSHIT

## THE VICE PRESIDENT'S TOWNHOUSE

MAY 13 (12:20 A.M.)

Romana Clay had caught me in the middle of my eighth rewrite of the Vice President's withdrawal statement, which turned out to be an all-night job. Or would have been if she hadn't called.

My initial reaction was that she'd been clued by a White House source that the Vice President was being dumped, and had tracked him down for an exclusive. It never occurred to me that she and Bully might be giving new meaning to the media term one-on-one. I was still under the impression that his taste in extramarital sex ran to patrician bluebloods—the discreet wives and daughters of America's ruling dynasties. But when I saw Romana at the top of the townhouse stairs in a flesh-colored peignoir, things fell into place: on one of the most critical nights of his career, Bully Vandercleve had decided to salve his wounded ego by bedding down the doyenne of network political correspondents.

So the rumors were true. Washington logic: In real life, the wife is always the last to know; in politics, it's the press secretary.

"Thank God you're here, Frank," she said, taking my hand

and leading me toward the master bedroom. "It's been a night-mare."

For the record, I am not much into reliving bad scenes; which is to say, I can take my trauma or leave it. Once, as a witness to a mugging (my own, near Capitol Hill), I blew the prosecutor's case when at the police lineup I went blank on whether the assailant was a swarthy mesomorph or a Teutonic ectomorph. All of which is to explain why, in recalling the scene in the bedroom that night, only two items stand out in my memory: first, the sound of the air conditioner going full-bore, rippling the Porthault sheets on the king-size brass bed; second, the beatific smile on the Vice President's face when Romana Clay lifted the top sheet.

Good TV reporter that she was, Romana didn't say a word, letting the picture tell the story; which was that Stewart Bulloch (Bully) Vandercleve—Vice President, former Governor, ex-Ambassador, one-time Secretary of Defense, erstwhile perennial candidate for the Republican presidential nomination—had died blissfully, at age fifty-nine, in carnal arrest.

Pause here for a credibility check: If the Bully Vandercleve who appears in the preceding scene—arrogant, self-indulgent, profane—doesn't match your impression of the Vice President, I take full credit. That just means I've earned my pay as his chief image maker over the past fifteen years.

No doubt you have in your media-jaded mind's eye the image of a modest, albeit excessively rich Bully, the perfect product of enlightened third-generation American capitalism: a compulsive philanthropist generous to those who labor in God's vineyards; a compassionate public servant sensitive to the needs of those less fortunate than he—what Bully called the poor slobs of the earth, as in "Lee, work up some remarks for the poor slobs of *(fill in the appropriate inner city ghetto, blue-collar district, or during foreign travels, Third World village)."*

That was Bully Vandercleve's contrived public image. Privately, however, my patron was a man of two minds: the first, driven by a WASPish upper-class need to Do Good by His Fellow Man (within Fiscal Reason, of course); the second, by a pagan impulse to enjoy life to the fullest, which to him meant paternalizing and/or dominating everything he could lay hands on.

Our paths first crossed when I was a young political animal working for Madvig & Beaumont, the PR firm handling his maiden campaign for governor. My mentor at the time was the agency's senior partner, a natty, diminutive Claude Rains look-alike named Phil Madvig. I was in the candidate's suite on election night, sipping Dom Perignon and nibbling Beluga while waiting for the opponent to concede, when old man Madvig drew me aside, raised his glass, and told me my ship had arrived.

"Congratulations, Frankie," he said, as we tipped crystal. "We're fifty-four percent ahead in the raw vote, fifty-seven percent projected. The upstate boxes are just coming in."

"A landslide!" I exclaimed (for I was still young and exuberant). "It only goes to show—"

"I'm not finished," said Madvig, holding up an instructive finger. "The client says he's impressed with your work. So impressed he wants to take you with him to Albany."

I was baffled. Aside from writing press releases on the weekly speaking schedule, my sole contribution to the campaign had been the giveaway shtick at Jewish precinct rallies: fortune bagels with a message baked inside, on a miniature talis: VANDERCLEVE: A MENSCH FOR THE TIMES.

Madvig saw my stunned expression and read my thoughts. "Have you heard the returns from the Jewish boxes?" he asked. "We're breaking fifty-fifty. Given the client's Middle East business connections, plus the fact that our opponent's the mayor of New York, it's a bloody mitzvah." Standing on tiptoe, he reached up and placed an avuncular hand on my shoulder. "Vandercleve is convinced the bagels swung it."

"The *bagels?*" I blurted. "That's absurd."

Now Madvig, still on tiptoes, was whispering conspiratorially into my ear. "Agreed," he said. "But the client believes it, so why quibble?"

A waiter passed, refilling our half-empty goblets. After a ceremonial clink, my mentor took a sip, smacked his lips, and proceeded with what promised to be my baccalaureate lesson in his school of political survival.

"Besides," he said, "who's to say the bagels *didn't* swing it? Stranger things have happened in American politics. My very first client, Thomas Dewey, lost the presidency because he wouldn't follow my advice and get rid of that damned mustache. Stubborn bastard, Dewey. Said it was a matter of principle." Madvig's face took on a look of rueful nostalgia. "You know, Frankie, I've always wanted my own President." He sighed. "One shave, we could've swept the country." He shrugged. "But that's history." He jabbed my pectoral with a manicured finger. "Never forget what I taught you, Frankie, the first rule of political PR."

*"What the client wants,"* I recited by rote, *"the client gets."*

"Good show," beamed Madvig, as we raised goblets one last time. *"What the client wants, the client gets*—especially when he's Bully Vandercleve, the richest politician in America." He drained his glass, set it on a nearby end table, and clasped my free hand in both of his. *"Mazel tov,* Frankie," he said, his eyes welling in tutorial pride. "When you get to Albany, don't forget your old mentor."

Thirty minutes later I got word from the client himself. The opponent had finally conceded, and as the governor-elect readied himself for the trip to the downstairs ballroom to face the cameras and crowd, he grabbed me by the elbow as he headed for the john. It was there, while Bully Vandercleve took his last leak as a member of the private sector, that he asked me to be his press secretary.

I accepted on the spot. The governor-elect nodded, zipped up his pants, washed, then held out his hands, waiting for something. A towel. He was waiting for a towel. I pulled one off the rack and gave it to him. After drying his hands, he gave it back. I dropped it down the chute. It was my first lesson in alter-egoing for the richest politician in America.

As governors go, Bully wasn't bad, considering he spent ninety percent of his time running for President. It's in the books: three losing campaigns in twelve years, enough to make him routine fodder for David Letterman's opening monologues. Not that Bully ran bad races—God knows he spent the money—but his timing was never quite right. As a moderate conservative he was too moderate for Republican conservatives the first time out, and too conservative for Republican moderates four years later. Then, the morning after his third convention loss, he got the call from the presidential nominee offering him the runner-up spot on the national ticket.

He snapped it up; though for a Type-A overachiever, the Vice Presidency is the worst kind of career move. Under the Constitution the only thing the job calls for is waiting: waiting for the President to die or be impeached; waiting for the Senate to wind up in a tie vote so the Vice President can break it.

That's all the Vice Presidency is about—waiting. Everything else is make-work. Like chairing the President's Special Commission on Territorial Reform (which took Bully to Guam in August). Or attending state funerals (which took him to Iceland in December). Or filling in at some political/cultural event that the President, for one reason or another, can't make (like the East Passaic Young Republican Pasta Festival).

A year on the job, waiting, waiting, waiting, and Bully was ready to climb the EOB walls. It was only a matter of time before he started looking for ways to drain his Type-A batteries.

It was golf and tennis during the daylight hours, indoor recreation after dark. That went on for the second and better part of his third year in office, until the incident at the Sun Devil Pro-Am. I screwed up on that one, letting him pose in a clubhouse shot with half a dozen Southwest dude ranchers and an angel-faced blonde palmed off as Miss Arizona Commerce, which turned out to be a euphemism for the feature attraction at a Scottsdale strip joint. The *Enquirer* (cropping everyone else out of the photo) ran the beaming twosome on its cover page, with the caption, "Who's the Pro and Who's the Am?" Which led Jack Anderson to check into Bully's schedule for the previous six months: five golf tournaments, three trips to Palm Springs, two to St. Bart's, and a fortnight cruise aboard Bill Buckley's *Cyrano II*.

Jack tagged him "the Dilettante Veep." And there he was, back in Letterman's nightly monologue.

DAVID LETTERMAN: "Have you heard the latest on Bully Vandercleve? Poor guy. He went to a strip joint and a golf tournament broke out."

It was then that Bully went into a dark funk, cutting public appearances to the bone, showing up at the office only to shuffle papers, play solitaire, and bitch about news leaks from the White House that he'd be dumped from the ticket.

"That could be a blessing," I told him, trying to look at the bright side.

"Not necessarily," he replied, eyeing the cards he'd dealt himself. "You can't tell in this job." He slipped the queen of hearts over the king of clubs. *"Anything* can happen."

Live in Washington long enough and even the obvious becomes obscure: I'd forgotten there's one state funeral that Type-A Vice Presidents don't necessarily mind attending. Given a sixty-seven-year-old President, Bully had incentive enough to hold on. Not to mention that being dumped would mean a return to private life, ending up as a resident has-been on Sunday talk shows.

So there he was—arrogant, self-indulgent, profane—when it all came down on him that morning in May: getting invited to breakfast with the President, finding out that the White House leakers were right. His political career had reached dead end.

Recovering my wits in the townhouse with Romana Clay, I remembered the very last order he gave me, after I'd returned to my office and begun drafting his withdrawal statement: "Don't rupture yourself, Frank," he phoned to say. "I don't need Washington's Farewell Address. Only a few bromides for the road."

# THE VICE PRESIDENT'S TOWNHOUSE

## MAY 13 (3:15 A.M.)

"You heard me the first time, Lee."

Having changed out of the peignoir and regained her composure, Romana Clay was stretched out on a lounge chair in dark slacks and a black-and-white sweater, her Gucci-booted feet propped on a glass table. "I'm not moving," she said, breathing smoke from a Dunhill cigarillo, "until those Secret Service creeps get word from the White House."

I checked my watch. Three-fifteen. Three hours had passed since my arrival, and the body of the Vice President of the United States was still cooling between sheets in the next room while his favorite TV correspondent and I argued over whether to let the protective detail outside know what had happened. In a town where reputations, good and bad, always exceed reality, Romana was proving an exception to the rule—as cool and tough as advertised.

*Romana Clay:* According to the cover story in *TV Guide,* she was born Romana Adele Klepperman, a child of complex heritage, her father a Bronx butcher who settled down South after World War Two, married a fetching Italian waitress, and opened what would become the best Italo-Jewish restaurant in Bessemer, Alabama. At age eighteen, impatient with TV-radio classes at the University in Tuscaloosa, an aggressive Romana headed for Manhattan and hired on as an assistant to one Sidney Falco, a show-biz flack with a client list that included a superstar episodically called to Washington to testify before anticrime committees.

It was during one such episode, while she was handing out press statements on Capitol Hill, that Romana's dark-eyed beauty and piquant Southern accent caught the eye and ear of a network bureau chief. Between committee sessions, they talked over career moves. He advised that she Anglicize her surname, abandon Manhattan, and move into his Watergate apartment. She followed his first two suggestions but turned him down on the third. He persisted; she hung tough; he met her terms: three months later they were married by a justice of the peace in Hagerstown, Maryland. Two weeks after that, Romana Clay joined the bureau as a cub reporter on Capitol Hill.

But not for long. Within eighteen months she was doing stand-ups on the White House north lawn for the nightly news. From that she moved to the chopper shift, with the choice assignment of bellowing questions at the President as he walked to and from his helicopter, Marine One. Her first day on the shift she showed up with a bullhorn and drowned out an aging Sam Donaldson. From that moment on, the old pros in the press corps knew they were up against a real competitor. Within two years she'd earned media star status by breaking stories on the Leffingwell Massacre and cost overruns on repainting the White House, not to mention wheedling an exclusive interview with the President's allergist. By the time she split with her producer-husband—jumping to a rival network in the process—Romana Clay had joined that elite group of Washington journalists who play as big a role in shaping as in reporting the news.

Inside stories were her specialty. Nobody worked harder at cultivating sources for possible news leads or leaks. Once a month she'd flatter me with a phone call, asking what was going on in the VP's office. "Frank," she'd purr before signing off, "we simply *must* do a lunch."

Needless to say, it was one of those Washington lunches that never got done, since a Vice President's press secretary isn't anyone a front-row journalist wants to be seen with midday at Maison Blanche or the Occidental, unless, of course, the President is being given the last rites. In any event, even her phone calls turned out to be conversational byplay. She obviously had far better access to what was going on in the Vice President's office than I did.

Bully and Romie: it had to be the best-kept Washington cover-up of its kind since JFK and Judith Exner. Incredible. The mere logistics of moving a celebrity squeeze in and out of the Vice President's townhouse without being noticed were awesome. Conclusive proof, I assured Romie, that they don't call it the Secret Service for nothing.

"Trust me," I entreated (after failing to win her over with male bluster). "The Service would never do or say anything to hurt the Vice President's reputation."

She crushed out her cigarillo, viewed me with what I took to be a patronizing glance, then regarding herself in a compact mirror, mended her lipstick and touched up her hair—a model of pragmatism, if not grace, under pressure.

"Don't be an idiot," she said as she snapped her compact shut. "It's not *his* reputation I'm thinking about."

I have since had time to reflect on the way in which political sycophancy over an extended period can warp one's professional perspective. During our entire argument over whether we should notify Shelby and the Secret Service detail about Bully's death—a dialogue that lasted nearly half the night—not once did it occur to me that *her* good name was part of the PR mix. Romana Clay, network news superstar, wasn't about to stake her career on the judgment of a dead Vice President's press secretary.

Not that I could blame her. How, I asked myself, would Al Shelby react on learning that the Vice President he was sworn to protect had died on his watch, in the company of a member of the despised news media? Would he be discreet? Or would he suspect foul play, call in the paramedics, and roar off to Georgetown Hospital, sirens blaring? Could I guarantee that Romana wouldn't be detained as a material witness, pending further investigation?

Not likely, with Shelby in charge, which was why, when the last word had been said, we ended up doing it her way. First, I'd contact Regis Strong, using White House leverage to lid Shelby and the Service detail, then she'd take the back door out, before we broke the news to the country and world that Vice President Vandercleve had died, *requiescat in pacem,* alone at his townhouse while working into the night on affairs of state.

## 2

 FYI, there are two ways to reach a top-level Presidential staffer who has an unlisted home phone number: first, through civilian operators working the White House switchboard; second, through Army Signal, a 395 number known only to insiders. Considering the hour, I took the military route and no questions asked.

*Transcript, Tape No. 121-X, telephone conversation through Army Signal switchboard, between Frank Lee, press secretary to the Vice President, and Regis Strong, the President's chief of staff, 13 May (0445 hours).*

| | |
|---|---|
| SIGNAL: | This is Signal, may I help you? |
| FL: | This is Frank Lee. I'd like to speak to Regis Strong at his residence. |
| SIGNAL: | Who? |
| FL: | Regis Strong, the President's chief of— |
| SIGNAL: | No, sir. I mean, who's calling? |
| FL: | Oh. Frank Lee, the Vice President's press secretary. I need to speak— |
| SIGNAL: | One moment, sir. |
| SUPERVISOR: | Sergeant Haskell here. Who did you say you were? |
| FL: | Frank Lee. L-e-e. Look, Sergeant, I have an urgent call— |
| SUPERVISOR: | Lee? Lee. Oh yeah, listed right here. Vice President's press secretary. You say you want to speak to Mr. Strong? |
| FL: | Urgently. |
| SUPERVISOR: | One moment, Mr. Lee, we'll put you through. |
| VOICE: | Hello? |
| SIGNAL: | Mrs. Strong? This is Signal. We have an urgent call for Mr. Strong from— |
| VOICE: | Wait a minute. Reg, it's the White House. Urgent. |
| RS: | *(Inaudible)* Strong speaking. Put the call through. |
| SIGNAL: | Yes, sir. |
| RS: | Mr. President? |
| FL: | Not exactly. It's Frank Lee. Sorry to wake you but— |
| RS: | Sweet Jesus. I'll be a— |
| FL: | Yes. Well, it's a matter of great— |

★ 21 ★

RS:     Do you know the *(expletive deleted)* time?

FL:     —urgency. We need to talk.

RS:     Lee. Vandercleve's press secretary, right?

FL:     A matter of urgency concerning the Vice President. But nothing we can talk about over the phone.

RS:     Lee, the last time I got called at this hour, it was the President asking if any word had come through on the Libyans testing a nuke in the Sahara. Do you read me?

FL:     Not quite.

RS:     Then let me put it this way. Sober up. If it still seems important and you're in any condition to talk, I'll be at my office at seven.

FL:     Seven, right. I'll be—hello? Hello?


## THE WHITE HOUSE WEST WING

### MAY 13 (7:00 A.M.)


Strong's office was on the second floor, the large corner suite once occupied by Mondale and Bush, with all the prestige that goes with a location just down the hall from the Oval Office.

I arrived promptly and took a seat in the reception room. There would be a wait, Mrs. Kaltenborn, the secretary, explained, "because Mr. Strong is going through NSC reports, screening overnight traffic from the embassies." I creased my brow to appear suitably awed, but at 7:10, while turning down her offer of a third cup of coffee, pressed my case about being there on a matter of urgency.

She addressed me with matronly eyes. "You look like you've

★ 22 ★

been through a wringer," she smiled. "Are you sure you can't use another cup of coffee? It's not the freeze-dried mess they serve in other offices around here. I grind it myself, a special blend, every morning."

"It's the envy of every office in the White House–EOB complex," I said craftily, extending my cup. "On second thought, I'll have another refill."

"The secret is two parts Mocha Java, one part Guatemalan," she said, pouring. "I'll see what I can do."

She disappeared, then reemerged moments later to escort me into the inner office. I seated myself in a straight-backed chair directly in Strong's line of vision if he'd been looking up, which he wasn't. Shuffling papers with one hand, he was making frenzied notes on a yellow legal pad with the other. One of the spiffiest dressers in official Washington, the chief of staff this morning wore a double-breasted blue serge suit with eagle-wing lapels, a white-on-white silk shirt, and a subdued power-red tie.

I waited until the secretary left the room. "We've got a problem," I blurted out. "A serious problem. It's—"

"Whatever it is"—Strong interrupted, chill blue eyes still fixed on the papers before him—"can wait till I'm finished."

One, three, five minutes passed. Finally: "Okay, let's have it. I'm due in the Oval Office and don't intend to keep the President waiting."

"It's about the Vice President," I began. "He's . . ."

"Yes?"

"Dead."

Strong looked up at me for the first time, his face suddenly flushed. "And that's why you woke me up at four in the morning," he said flatly. "Just to tell me that." He rose, shook his head, gathered his papers, and began walking briskly toward the door. "If you're looking for a new job," he added, hand on the knob, "leave your résumé with my secretary."

"Dead," I repeated, rising from my chair. "Around midnight. It happened at the townhouse. With Romana Clay."

"Clay?" Strong turned, squinting into the morning sunlight that

★ 23 ★

flooded the room. "What," he asked, bristling, "does *that* bitch have to do with it?"

"She's still at the townhouse and won't leave." I rushed the words. "Doesn't trust the Secret Service, so the body is still—"

"*What* body?"

"The Vice President's."

Strong released the doorknob. Head inclined, he studied me, then returned to his desk and picked up the phone. "Mrs. Kaltenborn, call Miss Duffy," he said. "Tell her to tell the President I'll be ten to twelve minutes late. Something's come up. Nothing to put off tomorrow's trip to Wisconsin, just something I have to deal with." He returned the phone to its cradle and sat down.

"So," he said, "you're not talking about what happened yesterday—Vandercleve getting the word that he's off the ticket. You mean, he's *dead* dead. Like he won't be holding a news conference this morning."

Much as I dislike his style, let me concede Regis Strong's talent for clearing away political underbrush. I assured him that barring resurrection, the Vice President wouldn't be holding a news conference this or any future morning.

"I see," he said, waving me to a sofa. "Sit down, Frank. Tell me about it in, say, twelve minutes or less."

*Excerpt of transcript, Tape 103-Y. Office conference between Regis Strong, WH chief of staff, and Frank Lee, VP press secretary, 13 May (0730 hours).*

RS: All right, the bottom line. Clay's still at the townhouse and nobody but she, you, and I know the Vice President's dead. The Secret Service doesn't know, and the Vandercleve family, they don't know. Only the three of us, right?

FL: Right. Nobody knows, and she won't leave the townhouse until the Secret Service gets orders from the White House that—

RS: No problem. All that takes is a call to the director of the Service. It's not exactly by the book, but the book wasn't written for what we have here. Do you get the big picture, Lee?

FL:    Big picture?

RS:    Lee, we're talking about the Presidency of the United States, the reason your boss was being dumped. He can't—couldn't help us in Tuesday's Wisconsin primary. As of yesterday the polls show Senator Stanton's running six points ahead of the President. Getting your boss off the ticket would have reversed those figures.

FL:    Well, he's off the ticket now.

RS:    There's off, and there's off. A dumped Vice President is one kind of off, a dead Vice President's another. Your boss's withdrawal would have put the Vice Presidency up for grabs. With the Number Two spot open, we planned to offer the VP nomination to Governor Kleck, quid pro quo for his endorsement. Kleck's as far left as Stanton. His support could pull in enough granola liberals to win Tuesday. But now we're in a bind.

FL:    A bind?

RS:    A bind, because now we don't have a lame duck, we've got a dead duck. The Vice Presidency is vacant, so the Twenty-fifth Amendment takes over.

FL:    Twenty-fifth Amendment?

RS:    Agnew, remember? The Vice President resigns—or dies—so the President has to send a name up to Congress to fill the vacancy. With your boss dead, we can't just *promise* Kleck we'll put his name up at the convention. The job's open, so we'd have to *give* it to him. Not next January but now.

FL:    So where's the bind? If you want Kleck as Vice President—

RS:    Who said anybody wants that *(expletive deleted)* to be Vice President? Watch my lips: I said we'd *promise* the nomination to get his endorsement before Tuesday's primary. After Tuesday, *(expletive deleted)* him.

FL: Jesus, you play hardball.

RS: Negative, Lee. Promising jerkwater pols the Vice Presidency and not delivering is an old American political custom. The only difference is, we're doing it during primary season, not at the convention. Hardball is this: You're not telling anybody your boss is dead. Not until we do our deal with Kleck. Not till Tuesday or Wednesday, when the votes are in.

FL: I don't follow.

RS: You want a diagram? As far as the world knows, Vice President Vandercleve is still alive, right?

FL: *(Inaudible)*

RS: That means the President can still go to Wisconsin, tell Kleck we're dumping Vandercleve, and the Vice Presidential nomination's coming open. That's all it'll take to get Kleck's endorsement. It'd be tidier with your boss alive, announcing his withdrawal at a press conference, but it can still work.

FL: I can't believe—

RS: Seventy-two hours, Lee, that's all we need. Instead of telling the world the Vice President's dead at noon today, you hold off till noon Tuesday. By that time we've got Kleck's backing and Wisconsin bagged.

FL: Let me get this straight—

RS: I'm running late, Lee. Sit here, have another cup of Mrs. K.'s coffee, think about it. Think about the Presidency, the future of the Free World, the Vandercleve family's feelings. Think how awful it would be if somebody leaked the real story of your boss's last hours. Think big picture, Lee, always think the big picture.

Go ahead, second guess me. But remember, I only had fifteen minutes to make up my mind before Strong returned from the Oval Office. A heart-to-heart with my professional guru was in order, but as luck would have it Phil Madvig was in London, still cleaning up the PR mess around Buckingham Palace after Chuck and Di's ugly custody fight. Still, Madvig got through to me. Floating on my sixth coffee of the A.M., I suddenly knew, in a flash of transatlantic telepathy, just what my old mentor would recommend:

*"What the client wants,"* he'd say, *"the client gets."*

It all came down to what Bully Vandercleve would have wanted, and on that count the call wasn't even close. Bully disliked the President, but he *despised* Buzz Stanton, because the Senator backed his first two runs for the White House but turned coat to oppose him the third time around. A fellow Princetonian, too. Bully was first mystified, then outraged.

What had happened was that on one particular swing through south Florida, my client's political outreach had gathered in Felicia Stanton, the Senator's nubile wife. For Bully, the episode was no more than a matinee performance between speeches, one of dozens during the campaign. But Stanton saw it otherwise; to the extent that, as Chairman of the Select Committee on Investment Fraud, he slapped a *subpoena duces tecum* on C. Foster Abel, not only the venerable dean of Wall Street barristers but also the chief investor for Bully's blind trust.

No doubt about it—if withholding news of his own demise for a few news cycles could zap Buzz Stanton in Wisconsin, Bully would want me to see the big picture. Besides, what were my options? To call Strong's bluff? Easy to say, but I knew it was no bluff. How had Bully put it? That he was to the manner born and the President had had to wait tables to put himself through some second-rate law school?

The President's chief of staff harbored the same plebian resentment as his boss. First and foremost, Regis Strong was out to lock up the President's renomination by winning in Wisconsin. But next to that—a close second—he would have relished letting the world know how Stewart Bulloch Vandercleve, the high-and-mighty patrician, had died with his boots off.

# THE VICE PRESIDENT'S RESIDENCE

## MAY 13 (10:00 A.M.)

The big picture. Strong lifted the phone, called the Director of the Service, and pulled Al Shelby's detail off the townhouse beat. "It's a done deal," he said after he hung up. "Now the ball's in your court." West Wing clichés ringing in my ears, I headed out the door.

Bully's weekend plans had been free-fall, no public appearances scheduled. That meant the first forty-eight hours were no problem. Except, of course, the problem of dealing with the Second Lady. After ten years of marriage to the world's richest political womanizer, Cissy Vandercleve was inured to her husband's overnight capers. But a whole weekend away from the nest? That would have been too much for her to swallow. Cissy, to say the least, wasn't shy. She'd be calling around, asking questions.

*Mildred Mastern Vandercleve:* She'd first met Bully in San Diego, not long after his second presidential campaign. When they were introduced—at a Republican fund-raiser where Bully was guest speaker—she was in her early thirties. Flowing red hair, hot hazel eyes, French vanilla complexion. What Bully liked to call "a second-looker." Not a stunner but a woman you'd look at twice in a crowded room. And, as it developed, a woman totally bored with a stale marriage to a La Jolla real estate developer.

In short, just the kind of off-duty diversion Governor Vandercleve was second-looking for on his trips to the West Coast.

What was different about the way Bully's diversion with Cissy got started—different, that is, from other on-the-road diversions—was that if Patricia Vandercleve hadn't been on that particular trip, her husband would never have met her successor. True, somewhere down the campaign trail—Bully being Bully and spouse switching being acceptable in American politics since the 1960s—he'd have met some other young woman, as hot-eyed and involved as the first Mrs. Vandercleve was gelid-eyed and detached.

But it happened at a reception in the grand ballroom of the Del Coronado Hotel, when Patricia Vandercleve ran into an ex–Sweet Briar classmate, one Zelda Westheimer, who proceeded to introduce the governor and his wife to her niece, Cissy.

Bully took one look, then a second, smiled—his high-octane smile—and asked the young woman whether she, like her aunt, had gone to Sweet Briar. "Stanford," she replied. "Government studies, cum laude. And I'm not much for small talk." With that she plunged elbow-deep into a pizza-sized Louis Vuitton handbag and pulled out a petition, furled tight by three intertwined red, white, and blue ribbons.

"You'll have to excuse my wife," squeaked the real estate developer, doing a Rodney Dangerfield finger-roll with his shirt collar. "If it's not one crusade, it's another. Last month—"

"I hardly need *you* to excuse *me,* Lester," snapped the future Second Lady, thrusting her petition on a line between Bully's clavicle and his mouth—which was still fixed, to everyone's surprise (including mine) in a broad grin. "Has it ever occurred to you, Governor," she was saying, "that while *we* make up fifty-three point six percent of the adult population of America, only *one* commemorative stamp in *thirty* is set aside for women?"

"Only one in thirty?" cried Bully, smile giving way to a look of feigned incredulity. "Why that's . . . *outrageous!"* The political womanizer-in-action, homing in on a target of opportunity. He handed me his Perrier and took up the petition, which he commenced to de-ribbon, unfurl, and read, against an audio background of muted gasps and clucking tongues, though Patricia Vandercleve, the patrician wife in action, merely shriveled her ex-classmate Zelda with a frigid glance.

Bully signed on, no staff advice sought or advanced. All I did was furnish the Scripto, with the petitioner herself supplying the upper back on which Governor Vandercleve affixed his name, beneath those of two other governors, three U.S. senators, nine congressmen, and the acting chairman of the Board of Supervisors of Orange County, California.

"Don't get an ulcer," he reassured me in the limo en route to the airport. "It's a dead-ender." Meaning, the signature wouldn't come back to haunt us because the petition was going nowhere. And he was right. As even the most casual philatelist knows, the campaign to honor the literary *oeuvre* of Ayn Rand with a commemorative stamp fell well short of its goal. But Bully's signature obviously served *his* purpose. After that trip our visits to California to take second-looks at Cissy the Petitioner became more frequent.

We would arrive in San Diego, L.A., San Francisco, and she'd be waiting at the hotel, cause-of-the-month in hand, everything from Save the Pelicans to Self-Determination for Bessarabia. Bully would sign, then they'd move on to other things. The real estate developer? He didn't seem to mind. *Droit du seigneur,* bourgeois American–style: Any man can be cuckolded, but not every man can say he was cuckolded by a Vandercleve.

A year after their first meeting, Cissy got her divorce: no kids, no problem. Twelve months after that, Bully made his break. As such things go—thirty-one years of marriage, three grown children—the split was civilized. Still, as a PR specialist trained in the Madvig tradition, I was against the divorce and even more opposed to his remarrying a younger woman. New Morality to the contrary, I had serious doubts about wife switching in the middle of the political stream.

At times, however, my traditional instincts prove wrong. After three months of post-nuptial polling, I began to appreciate the plusses Cissy Vandercleve brought to the governor's mansion. Whatever we'd lost in late-middle-age women's votes was more than made up by Cissy's popularity among thirty-five-and-under activists. And more—while the first Mrs. Vandercleve had an aristocrat's indifference to her husband's profession, the second was a political junkie. Cissy loved the game, whether hosting lawn picnics at the mansion, filling in for Bully on speaking engagements he couldn't make, or doing the loyal wife's stand-up bit at political rallies, where the Governor invariably introduced her as "my strong right arm."

The Freudian joke was that Bully was left-handed. His strong right arm was fine for the mansion, but he could no more stay faithful to one woman than he could resist chasing the presidency.

So that in time, Cissy Vandercleve, like her aristocratic predecessor, would learn to live with (though never accept) her husband's chronic womanizing.

"This Clay person," the Second Lady was saying. "Is she the one with the bovine eyes I catch on the morning news?"

"She does the evening news," I corrected. "Stand-ups on the White House north lawn."

"Evening news," the Second Lady repeated. Still drenched from an early morning session on the tennis court, she ran a damp towel across her throat. "Right. I remember now. The one with the bullhorn—"

I nodded.

"—and the cut-rate nose job."

I let it pass. I'd arrived at the residence a little before ten. Cissy was on the court, baselining a local club pro, who seemed relieved to zip up his racket and call it a day's work. The two of us—she bicycling, me hustling to keep pace—headed for the residence, the tinted-white Victorian house anchored halfway up Naval Observatory Hill. By the time we arrived and settled down on the veranda (10:07), I'd brought her up to speed, the whole story—give or take a few graphic details. All in all, she took the news rather well. Certainly better than the first Mrs. Vandercleve would have. The only thing that surprised her was the identity of her husband's last bedmate.

"I always knew Bully would die in the sack," she said, pressing the towel against the nape of her neck. "Either there or at Ford's Theater, shot by a jealous husband. But *Romie Clay?* I would've thought she was a bit overripe for his tastes."

She shrugged, tossed the towel aside, and moved into a different gear. *"So,* Mr. Alter Ego," she said, "how does the ever-faithful flack put a positive spin on *this* one?"

"The White House thinks we'll need to adjust the time a little," I replied.

"Till noon?" She reached over and checked my Swatch. "Say he passed away after a heavy lunch?"

"Noon, right, that sounds good," I said. "Say, noon Tuesday."

"Tuesday?"

"Let me explain—"

"Lee," she said, "I'm in no mood for any of your horse pucky."

"No horse pucky at all," I replied. "It's the Wisconsin primary. A straight political trade-off: the White House gets to use the vice presidential nomination as bait; we get to save the Vice President's good name."

The *Vice President's* good name! I'd said it again, and by the glare coming off those hot hazel eyes it was clear I'd made the same sycophant's mistake with Bully's wife that I'd made with his mistress. But there was still time to recoup. "More important," I added, "to save *you* the problem of having to face reporters if word ever got out that your husband had died—"

She held up her hand. The glare dissolved. "I get the picture," she said. The big picture, which in her case meant that since the manner of her husband's demise required some form of deception anyway, a seventy-two-hour delay was merely a difference in degree, not kind.

So it all fell into place: the Second Lady would handle the Vice President's absence with his office staff, his family, and close friends. No big PR problem there. His Sunday doubles match with old college chums could easily be shredded. She'd call the office Monday morning to tell McCluskey that the Vice President was under the weather and, with nothing important on his schedule, he didn't plan to come in. As for the family, the oldest son practiced medicine in Chicago and hadn't spoken to his father since the divorce and remarriage; a second, brain-burned, son was in a commune in Montana; a rebellious daughter had left home at eighteen to take up a career as a rock singer. There were also two brothers, a sister, and assorted other relatives and friends who might try to reach him; but if they did, Cissy Vandercleve would simply say the Vice President was away and out of touch. In just those words.

Hardly a lie, by modern political standards; only a matter, as Regis Strong had put it, of making a public figure's untimely death timely.

# THE PRESS SECRETARY'S FAMILY ROOM
## MAY 14 (7:00 A.M.)

Still half asleep, sipping instant and scanning the morning papers, I reflexively waited for the call that wouldn't come.

It had been Bully's Sunday habit to rise early, read the general news, business, and sports sections of *The New York Times* and *Washington Post,* then touch base with his press secretary to find out what the pundits were saying in the opinion section. This allowed him to answer truthfully, if asked about some critical editorial or column, that he wouldn't comment on it because he hadn't read it.

The opinion sections that Sabbath were given over to the upcoming Wisconsin primaries. Since the Opposition party had no fewer than twenty-three presidential candidates in the field (including three Kennedys, two Roosevelts, and an unknown running as "The Masked Marvel"), the pundits, following the course of least confusion, were focusing on the Republican race. In his column on the *Post* Op-Ed page, Mark Dyer, the venerated dean of Washington political correspondents, wrote that the Republican outcome in Wisconsin hinged on (1) whether Governor Kleck stayed on the fence or threw his support to the President, and (2) the outcome of Monday's televised debate between the President and Senator Stanton.

Both papers also featured public opinion polls. According to the *Post*/ABC survey, Stanton was leading the President in Wisconsin by four percentage points. The *Times*/CBS poll showed Stanton ahead by seven. Both polls agreed that the Senator's numbers had grown because of the attention he was getting as chairman of the special committee investigating Wall Street scams prevalent since the mid-1980s. The President, according to the surveys, was perceived as "soft on Wall Street."

Nowhere in any of these items was there any mention of the Vice President. Except for a standard Bottoms-Colfax column predicting he'd be dumped, it really wasn't that bad a Sunday in Vice Presidential coverage, which isn't to say that Bully Vandercleve, if alive, would have seen things that way. The Bottoms-Colfax column (though old boilerplate copy) would have been enough to ruin his (and my) Sunday. If it happened to be one of those mornings when his blood sugar was low, he might even have given me orders to lodge complaints with the syndicate that ran Bottoms-Colfax, its attorney of record, and the principal supplier of newsprint for all papers carrying the column.

Patiently, I'd have pointed out that it was only 4:00 A.M. in L.A., where the syndicate was located, *ergo,* a call to their editor might prove counterproductive; agitated, he'd have replied he didn't care what time it was, just put the goddamned call in; reluctantly, I'd have said, "Have it your way"; finally, I'd have ignored the entire conversation, knowing he'd forget the order by Monday morning.

Madvig's PR Rule Number two: *If the client knew what was good for him, he wouldn't need a PR man in the first place.*

Based on my seventeen years with the man, that's the way it would have gone if Bully were still around. But he wasn't. My Sundays would never be the same.

FYI, this seems as good a place as any to plug in the details of my personal life at that particular point in time.

The quantitative data: There was (and barring some late-breaking news development, still is) one wife, Maureen, called Mo, who that Sunday A.M. was upstairs, sleeping off a long-winded night at a party fund-raiser; one schizoid mutt, called Abelard, the product of a pit bull seduced by a prize French poodle; a vagabond cat called Heloise, but who in fact answered to no name; an alarmingly precocious son, Tommy, who called himself Che and, having passed through a mantra-chanting stage at age fifteen, had progressed from puerile Zen Buddhism to puerile Marxism, a form of teenage metamorphosis (according to our child psychologist) not unusual in the rebellious progeny of a mixed marriage.

Oh, yes, about Mo . . . that party fund-raiser, you see, featured speeches by all twenty-three presidential candidates of the Opposition party, a euphemism I frequently rely on (according to our marriage counselor) to sublimate the squalid fact that my wife is a D——t. Always has been, going back to our undergraduate days at Syracuse, where I majored in journalism and she was pre-law.

Not that Mo hasn't changed. When we first met at an exhibition game, early spring of seventy-two (Mets 11, Syracuse Orangemen 2), she was a mere rank-and-file D——t. Now she's a hardened pro, working for a law firm (Coventry, O'Boyle & Wisenheimer) that counts among its pro bono clients the Center for Meaningful Liberal Alternatives and the Opposition—no, let me spit it out—*Democratic* National Committee.

And how, you ask, does the alter ego of a Republican Vice President get and stay tied to a Democratic partisan who, to this day, admits to having voted for George McGovern as a *write-in* in 1988? Pure chemistry. Not simply physical attraction (which our counselor, himself three times married, warns can only go so far), but a cosmic common interest which, from the start, precluded any intrusion of mundane political difference—to-wit, a shared passion for the destiny of the New York Mets.

Truth is, the subject of politics came up only once during our thirteen months of ardent courtship. Mo appeared one morning, casually sporting a McGovern bumper sticker on back of her sixty-eight VW. Stung, I showed up that evening in a coat, tie, and vest, wearing an American flag lapel pin just below my Nixon-Agnew button. She glared. I sneered. We argued, late into the night; until, following a quarter hour of chilling silence, she, to her credit, saw the light that I, in my petty piqué, had failed to see. Leaning in, she pecked me, oh so gently, on the right cheek (my good side, mediagenically speaking), then whispered—the warm breath of reason breaking the ice—"Frank, *Frank*. Between Mets fans, what difference does it make *who's* President of the United States?"

Easter break of seventy-three we eloped to Tampa and were married by a Florida justice of the peace, just before the final spring training game of the year (Mets 5, Reds 3). Our first-and-only-born, Thomas Seaver Lee, arrived—eight pounds, five ounces, Mo's blue eyes, my receding hairline—four seasons later. A Yankee year, and to compound dismal harbingers, the boy was left-handed, but *right*-brained, our child psychologist assured us: a Mensa-certified 175-IQ phenom who, in his worst moments of teenage rebellion, wears Cardinal red.

The phone was ringing . . . *ringing* . . . RINGING!

Halfway through a Sunday *Times* thinkpiece by former Mayor Koch ("Don't Say I Didn't Warn You!") I'd dozed off, somewhere between a dangling denunciation and a split rebuke. Jolted awake, I lunged for the receiver, sending cold coffee across the room.

*"What the hell's going on, Lee?"*

Romie Clay, checking in. Once again, I'd overlooked her part of the PR equation and she didn't sound too pleased about it.

"Romie!" I managed, shaking the webs. "Where've you been?"

"Where've *I* been?" she replied, in the sandpaper tone I recalled from the last hours of our session at the townhouse. "You know my number, Lee, and if you don't, Signal does. There've been three news cycles with no announcement about our mutual friend. What's the story?"

The story . . . let's see now: Since she, of all people, knew about Bully, my immediate impulse was to fill her in on Wisconsin and the big picture. But wait. Though a charter accomplice, Romana Clay, after all, was a member of a bizarre breed with mixed loyalties and turbid motives, i.e., a White House reporter. As of that moment, the only people on the Need-to-Know list were Regis Strong, the Second Lady, me, and, of course, the President. Add the Director of the Secret Service, that made four. Throw in the skeleton Service unit detailed to "guard" the Vice President until we broke the news, that brought the NTK list to a dozen, at the most.

Question: Could Romana Clay, TV news superstar, be trusted with the big picture?

Answer: Not necessarily, but considering that one way or another, she'd learn the truth, what choice did I have? So I filled her in. Well . . . partly.

"Stay cool," I said, on my unctuous best PR behavior. "The announcement's coming. It's only a matter of time."

"What's that supposed to mean?"

"No big deal," I said, feigning nonchalance. "You'll know all there is to know come Tuesday."

Bad mistake. *Awful* mistake. Never say "know" to a reporter, old man Madvig once told me. It's the K-word, the red flag that sends them charging.

"Know?" she said. "I thought I already *knew*. Bully's dead, so what else is—?" An ill-boding pause. Then: "Tuesday, you say?"

"Day after tomorrow," I replied. "But, really, no big—"

"Tuesday! The Wisconsin primary! Lee, you *sonofabitch,* you and Strong have something working. *Why didn't you let me know?"*

"Know what?" I asked. "Hey, Romie, this is your pal, Frank, remember? We're on the same side."

"Like hell we are," she set me straight. "You're a flack, Lee, a lousy flack. And I'm a reporter, first, last, and always. When you get ready to make that announcement on Tuesday, *you* remember: I expect a full fifteen-minute—no, make that a twenty-minute— edge over the competition." Pause. "Or else."

And with that, she hung up.

*Or else?* I had no idea what she meant, but whatever it was, I made a mental note that the Need-to-Know list had just grown by one.

Mo, dishevelled in an over-sized V-neck Mets shirt that reached her kneecaps, was up and stirring. Deep gray crescents rimmed her eyes, as if she'd spent half the night listening to twenty-three Democratic visions of America's future.

"It's early," I said. "I thought you'd sleep in after the orgy."

"So did I," she nodded, "but the phone woke me up." She took in the coffee stain that trailed across the floor. "The usual Sunday morning call?"

"The usual Sunday morning call," I replied, fumbling for the sports section. "Another bad Bottoms-Colfax column."

She yawned and shook her head. "Refill?" she asked, turning toward the kitchen.

"Yeah, thanks," I said, hastily scanning box scores. "Hey, hear this! Gooden pitched a two-hitter. . . ."

## THE VICE PRESIDENT'S PRESS OFFICE

MAY 15 (10:30 A.M.)

⭐ "What's with the strange hulks in the hall?"

Face burnished from yet another weekend of Ocean City rays, my deputy, Carla Braunschweig, hovered over the desk.

It was Monday morning, forty-eight hours down, twenty-four to go. All systems working: McCluskey, on hearing from the Second Lady that the VP was under the weather, assumed that's why he hadn't held his Saturday news conference. But I'd been wrong about one thing: Bully's schedule wasn't completely open. There was a 2:00 P.M. appointment with his barber that had to be canceled. The barber, Otto De Faye ("The Hairstylist of Presidents") was miffed, but other than that, no problems.

No problems; though I might have known there'd be some kind of encounter with Carla who, even on normal workdays, peppered me with questions. Pert, bright, and untouchable (married as she was to Number 75, Bruce Braunschweig, the Washington Redskins' 270-pound defensive tackle), Carla was hard to handle even as a novice, when she'd first joined my staff as a secretarial temp. An honors graduate of the Stanislavsky School of Method Stenography, she was one of those visceral office workers not satisfied merely to take dictation, type ninety words a minute, and shred documents on command. Carla had to understand motive, to grasp the existential meaning of her job.

I nonetheless ignored her question, focusing instead on a pink phone memo she handed me, one carrying a formidable media name, Ben Colfax. "When did the Prince of Darkness call?" I asked.

"Nine-oh-five this morning, just like it reads," she replied. "I asked, what's with the strange hulks in the hall?"

"No big deal. Just a new protective detail. What did Colfax want?"

"To talk about his TV interview with the boss this Friday. What was wrong with the old protective detail?"

"And just when did the Vice President commit to a TV interview with Colfax?" I countered. The conversation, you see, had at this point gone two-track, Carla headed in one direction, me in another.

"Since the Gridiron Dinner, when you got zonked and made the commitment. Colfax wanted him just before the big primaries, and you said fine. I thought it was a dumb idea at the time and still do. Now tell me: why the change in details?"

"Jesus, I'd forgotten all about it," I said, flapping the pink memo. "Keep Colfax off my back until I figure a copout."

"I follow no orders," she said, planting herself firmly in front of the desk, "until I know about the new hulks behind the shades."

I shrugged. "What's to know?" I said. "All Secret Service agents wear shades. It's part of the uniform."

"Indoors?"

She had a point. That *was* odd. But for the quick-witted flack, all is readily explainable. "It's a special unit shipped in from the West Coast," I dissembled. "L.A. office. A routine change, nothing more."

She came around the desk. "Would your routine change have anything to do with this call?" She handed me a second phone memo, this one bearing the formidable name of Sam Andreas, the Number One man on the Vice President's Secret Service detail. "Something strange is going on, Frank," she said. "What is it? Is the boss being dumped?"

The truth is that I never could con Carla, but the challenge was always there, sharpening my professional skills for the world outside, which I guess is why I hired her in the first place. Even the best of alter egos needs someone around to remind him of his limitations. Sooner or later, I'd have to level with her about the new protective detail.

But not just then. It would have to wait. Sam Andreas wanted to talk to me.

## GOLDBERG'S KOSHER DELI
### MAY 15 (NOON)

We met at Sam's favorite restaurant. Goldberg's is the midday antipode of the Palm a few blocks away. It's the place Washingtonians go for lunch when they *don't* want to be seen. There is no Mr. Goldberg, but the establishment bears that name because the proprietor, a Korean, had a business hunch that a place named Kim's Kosher Deli wouldn't cut the mustard on K Street.

If you don't recall Sam Andreas, let me refresh your memory: His was the dour Aegean countenance with the overgrown eyebrows, always peering over the Vice President's shoulder in news photos. It wasn't that Sam wanted his picture taken, only that he had the paranoid notion, based on a Hitchcock film he'd seen as a boy, that behind every camera lurks a potential assassin.

★ 40 ★

One night after his agents had been especially rough on some wire-service photographers, I argued the point in the Secret Service command post at the Carlyle, where Bully always stayed when visiting Manhattan. Sam heard me out, then went on to describe a scene in *Foreign Correspondent* where this European prime minister, with Joel McCrea looking on, got it between the eyes from a .38 hidden inside a tricked-up Leica.

"Right here." Sam pressed a square-tipped fingernail a quarter inch above his hummock nose. "There was blood everywhere. I was only nine at the time, but it made an indelible impression. I told myself, Andreas, the Good Lord put you here to save poor bastards like that."

"Sam, it was only a movie," I protested.

He shook his head. "Life," he replied in classic Athenian, "imitates art." And from that moment on I knew that in Sam Andreas I was dealing with more than your run-of-the-mill Secret Service paranoid.

This particular midday, Sam was a furrow-browed wreck. I'd never seen him quite that dour, but all things considered, it was understandable. He hadn't slept in thirty-six hours, not since getting word from the Director of the Secret Service that the remains of the Vice President he was sworn to protect were at that moment in a Wedgewood urn aboard a private Gulfstream IV, headed across the Great Plains. (Bully's express desire, written into his will: to be cremated and have his ashes strewn across his favorite ski slope, Number 5 at Keystone, Colorado.)

"Why didn't you contact *me* instead of Strong?" Sam wanted to know. I explained Romana Clay's irrational distrust of the Secret Service, but he wasn't buying. Paranoids, I've learned, have little empathy for the problems of other paranoids.

"Just because I was off-duty that night didn't mean you couldn't reach me," he continued, cupping a hand around his mouth to foil any lip-readers working the area. "That would've been the logical thing to do."

Logic: We were stashed in a back room booth at Goldberg's because Sam insisted there was no way we could talk within a two-block radius of the White House without being recorded.

"Everything and everybody's monitored," he confided, biting into an overdone knockwurst. "From the secretaries in the West Wing powder room to the placard freaks in Lafayette Square."

"Lafayette Square is wired?" I asked.

"Electronically surveilled," he corrected, licking a dollop of sauerkraut from his thumb. "A dish aimed from the Chamber of Commerce building on H Street."

"Funny," I said, "in three years of working together you never mentioned that."

"I never mentioned the Vice President and Romana Clay either," Sam said irritably. "But that was then, this is now, and the old rules don't apply."

A white-liveried waitress approached, mumbling apologies as she leaned across our table to refill the napkin dispenser. Sam eyed her like a mongoose measuring an asp. "You can't be too careful these days," he said, rattling the dispenser against his ear after the attendant moved on. Then: "Whose bright idea was it to burn the body?"

"It's called cremation," I replied. "He always said he wanted it that way, and the Second Lady agreed."

"Umm-hmm," Sam responded, nibbling the edge of a half-sour. "With no autopsy?"

"You tell me," I said. "Whatever your people decided."

"*Our* people?" The Aegean brow descended as Sam dropped the half-sour and shoved his sandwich to one side. "You mean Strong didn't tell you? We wouldn't touch this operation with a ten-foot cattle prod. Nossir."

"I'm not following," I said. "Are you telling me that the Secret Service is—"

"Off the assignment," said Sam. "Moving Al Shelby from the townhouse was one thing, but when the Director told me they wanted the Vandercleve file kept active posthumously, I said, 'Tell Strong to kiss my keister.' "

"And those agents in the hall today?"

"Those miserable shits aren't agents," snapped Sam. "They're Strong's Handymen."

"Strong's *what?*"

"Keep it down." Sam touched an index finger to his lips. "It's like I've always told you, Lee. You think you know it all, but what you don't know about this town could fill the Library of Congress. Which, by the way, is also bugged."

"Not agents?" I whispered, catching the paranoid ambience of the moment. "Then they're *ringers?*"

"Two years ago," explained Sam, "Strong decided Hertz needed a special paraintelligence unit to deal with covert crap no legitimate agency would touch. Like sifting through the garbage cans of Senators and newsies who make problems for the White House. Or unloading the body of a dead Vice President. Want to know how they did it?"

His eyes darted around the room. "Dressed as refrigerator repairmen. After Clay left, they came to the townhouse, put the VP's corpse into a Mitsubishi deep-freeze, and were gone by the time the cleaning lady arrived. Lucky she didn't show up early. As far as Strong's Handymen are concerned, two stiffs fit in a freezer easy as one."

Now it was my turn to shove a half-eaten Korean knockwurst to one side. "Ringers," I mused. "So Carla's instincts were right."

"Ex-spooks and FBI rejects," said Sam disdainfully. "Muscle-bound PIs from the West Coast. Beach bums from Laguna. Chuck Norris types that impress Regis Strong."

Another white uniform appeared, this one bent at the waist, mopping. Sam glanced at his digital. "It's past lunch hour, we're the only people in the joint," he said. "Let's take a walk."

FYI, in case you're not up to speed on Washington esoterica, *Hertz* is the government code for the President, *Avis* for the Vice President. There are two theories around town on how presidential code names are picked—*Searchlight* for Nixon, *Deacon* for Carter, *Rawhide* for Reagan. One theory has it that they're dreamed up by the same drone at the Weather Bureau who labels hurricanes. A second, conspiratorial theory is that an elite CIA think tank runs through all the options, A to Z, develops a short list, then draws the winner out of a hat—actually a green beret—in an arcane ritual held at Fort Myer once every four to eight years.

I once asked Sam Andreas which version was true. He told me, as a concerned paranoid friend, that it was none of my god-damned business.

## K STREET

MAY 15 (2:30 P.M.)

"You're in over your head, you know," Sam admonished me as we headed back to the White House–EOB. "The Service won't blow the whistle because of the VP's good name. But what you're into here, friend, is heavy-duty fraud."

"Lighten up, Sam." I patted him on the shoulder, feeling the bulge of his holster strap. "It'll be all over in twenty-four hours." A reassuring thought. Hearing that Strong had sent in a phony detail to impersonate the Secret Service had shaken me up.

"You mean, over with the Wisconsin primary?" He unwrapped a panatela and neatly excised the tip with a pocket knife. "You're sure about that?"

"Positive," I replied. "When Hertz wins Wisconsin, it's history. All we're talking about, really, is a four-day delay. Four days in May. He died Friday, we make the announcement tomorrow."

"Saying?" Sam gimlet-eyed an upscale street vendor selling designer-label merchandise, then cupped his hand against the wind to light his cigar.

"That Vice President Vandercleve died peacefully in his sleep. At the residence. Coronary occlusion. The medical records will bear it out."

"Oh?" The brows lifted. "What about Doc Irwin?" Irwin was the Navy physician who traveled with the Vice President.

"No problem," I said. "Irwin's been reassigned and the Vandercleve family doctor's been lined up to do the laundry. Time, place, cause of death. I'll explain there's no public funeral because

★ 44 ★

Bully always said he didn't want one. Just cremation and memorial services."

We stopped at the corner of 21st and F. Just outside the range, Sam informed me, of the Handymen's eavesdropping apparatus. The baroque gray façade of the Executive Office Building loomed over the eastern horizon.

"So you've got it all figured," Sam said, hunched forward to relight his cigar.

"All that matters," I replied.

"And if Hertz doesn't win in Wisconsin tomorrow?" he asked, pondering the ash end of his cigar. "Then what?"

I couldn't help laughing. "Sam," I said, clapping him on the holster strap, "you're a good friend and a great Secret Service agent. But as a political expert, you don't know squat. Hertz is a lock."

## AIR FORCE ONE, EN ROUTE TO WASHINGTON

MAY 15 (5:00 P.M.)

*The President was exultant. Quietly exultant. As he unwound in the semidarkness of his private cabin, tie loosened, shoes off, he sipped an old-fashioned, nibbled a carrot twist, and gazed down at the lights of Fort Wayne, Indiana, contemplating their larger meaning.*

*"Regis," he said to his chief of staff, "this has been one of the best days I've had in more than twenty years of campaigning, and I want to thank you for it. Magnificent staff work."*

*The chief of staff, poring over a computer printout by the dim light of the cabin desk, said nothing.*

*"There was the Kleck endorsement, the crowds, then the kiss planted on my cheek by that little girl who broke through the*

police lines to hand me those flowers. That touched me, Regis, truly touched me."

The President sipped his drink and dabbed his lips with a paper napkin bearing the Presidential seal. "That little girl," he said. "She was the real article, wasn't she?"

The chief of staff, absorbed in the printout, said nothing.

"Regis, I've asked a question," said the President. "That little—"

"If you're asking, was she a little girl or a midget, the answer, sir, is that she was a little girl," replied Strong, scanning a line of statistics with a ballpoint.

"That's not what I asked," said the President. "What I mean is, was her gesture genuine and not . . . and not just some cheap PR stunt concocted by our advance man. Something tells me it was genuine, you know? After a while, you can see it in their eyes, Regis. Feel it in your gut, the difference between the genuine and the phony. That little tyke, she meant it. Did you see her sign? It said We Luv You, Mr. Prezident . . . L-u-v . . . P-r-e-z—"

"She was a plant, sir," said Strong, flipping pages. "Her father's on the payroll of our Wisconsin finance chairman. Good advance work. Great advance work. They video-tested half a dozen kids, including professional models, and she won out on poise and mediageneity."

The President sat silent. He put his glass down and stared into the ink-blue sky beyond the cabin window. Finally: "You didn't have to tell me, you know. You, of all people, should understand that an American President—a man trapped in the lonely splendor of the most powerful office in the Free World—is entitled to a few illusions. I don't know what I'd do without you, Regis, but sometimes . . ." The President's voice trailed off. He reached for a carrot twist.

"I wouldn't have said anything, but you asked," replied Strong, eyes still fixed on the printout. "I never keep things from you."

"You see, Regis, I need my little illusions," said the President. "Need them because I have a vision. The vision that led me to take on this awesome burden. The vision that drives me, despite all personal sacrifice—"

Pages of printout in one hand, ballpoint in the other, Strong swung around to face the President. "Speaking of visions, sir," he said, "try this one on for size: the vision of a sitting President getting his ass whipped in Wisconsin on Tuesday."

The President, caught in midperoration, blinked through watery blue eyes. "You interrupted me, Regis," he said. "What's more, I don't think I heard you right. Ass whipped? What are you talking about?"

"What this survey tells us"—Strong began, rapping ballpoint to paper for emphasis—"is that there's been a major shift—"

"What are you talking about? You were there today, Regis," the President broke in, now on his feet. "You heard Kleck compare me to Lincoln, to Theodore Roosevelt. You saw the crowds, the sky over Madison filled with red, white, and blue balloons. You saw that, didn't you?"

"Yes, sir," replied Strong, "but—"

"Then what do you mean, 'ass whipped'?"

Strong chewed his lower lip and fixed his gaze on the printout. "You want it straight, sir?"

"Straight," said the President.

"All right, for starters, remember when I said it wasn't a good idea to debate Stanton the day before the primary—that it was a no-win situation?"

"So?"

"I wanted you to go to Madison, get Kleck's endorsement, then make Green Bay for a night rally and take off, back to Washington."

"So?"

"But our big butter-and-egg backers in Wisconsin, they had another idea. It's Cheese Festival Week in Madison, they said. A televised debate between the President and Senator Stanton at the fairground is just the ticket to pull in the crowds."

"Get to the point, Strong," said the President. "You know I don't like petty details. Just spell it out in one page."

"All right, one page," said Strong. "But I think, sir, you ought to sit down first."

The President sat down. He leaned over and began rummaging through a briefcase, his hand emerging with a thumb-size cylindrical case bearing a miniature Presidential seal.

"You were down six points going into Wisconsin," said Strong. "The Kleck endorsement figured to put you ahead. But the post-debate numbers say that four out of every five primary voters who saw the show thought Stanton won. Not just won, but won big. So even with Kleck's backing, we lost ground today. We came to Wisconsin down by six, we left down by nine."

"You're wrong, Regis," said the President, now gazing out the cabin window and regarding the lights of America—specifically Mansfield, Ohio—with newfound suspicion. "Dead wrong."

"It's not me talking, sir, it's the figures." Strong gingerly placed the survey printout on the President's lap. "Look for yourself. It's all there, in black and white."

"I don't trust these quickie polls," said the President, brushing the printout away. "What did they cover—four-hundred people in thirty minutes? Inaccurate, totally unscientific."

Strong retrieved the printout from the cabin floor. "I'd like to think so, Mr. President, but we've been using the same quickie polls for three years and they haven't been wrong yet," he said.

"Well, there's always a first time." The President sulked, his breathing now heavy. Then: "I won that frigging debate, Regis. Won it going away."

"Well, sir, the tracking numbers say otherwise," replied Strong. "Specifically, they say you blew the third question. The one on dairy prices."

The President swiveled about, a surprised look on his face. "I thought my answer to that question was outstanding," he said. "There was Stanton, beating around the bush, spewing numbers like a crazed calculator, rattling on about subsidies, consumer interests, all that hogwash. And I, I—"

Strong turned to a page in the survey. "Your precise words, Mr. President, were, I quote, 'We don't want a dairy farmer's price of milk, we don't want a consumer's price of milk, we want—"

"An American price of milk!" exclaimed the President.

"Right to the heart of the problem. A brilliant riposte, if you ask me."

"Unfortunately, sir, they didn't ask you. They asked four hundred thirty-two probable Wisconsin primary voters, including a hundred and twelve dairy farmers, who said—"

"I don't care to hear about it, Regis," said the President, turning toward the cabin window. "As far as I'm concerned, the day's been perfect. Let's just leave it that way." Perspiring, he dabbed at his brow with a handkerchief, then opened the small cylindrical case and plucked out a pea-size blue pill.

"Water?" asked Strong.

The President nodded. Strong poured lukewarm water from a desk carafe into a paper cup and handed it to him. The President washed the pill down, took another sip of water, then looked high into the night, avoiding eye contact with whatever Ohio village lay below. Strong turned his attention back to the printout. Suddenly:

"Vandercleve," said the President. "As long as we're talking about blowing things, Regis, tell me again why we didn't follow through on Vandercleve's public withdrawal. It seemed simple enough. We had our little breakfast. He agreed to hold a news conference the next morning. Tell me again, why didn't he?"

"Because he took sick that afternoon," said Strong, eyes riveted to the survey. "Some kind of allergy. But since we got Kleck's endorsement anyway—"

"Yes, but it would have been a lot simpler with Vandercleve withdrawing," said the President. He swung around to face his chief of staff. "You're sure he was sick? That there isn't something more to it?"

"Sir?"

"I mean," said the President, "are you sure Mr. High-and-Mighty isn't just being difficult? I don't trust him, Regis. Not one bit. We have another round of primaries coming up, and the sooner he withdraws, the better. Maybe the thing to do is call him in for another breakfast session. No, make it lunch. I can't stand looking at him early in the morning."

There were three quick, tentative raps on the cabin door.

"Who?" Strong called out.

"Cook," came the muffled response.

"Come," said Strong.

Harry Cook, the White House press secretary, entered to ask if the President was ready for his news conference when Air Force One landed in Washington.

"We're scrubbing the news conference," said Strong. "Going straight to the White House." The President, eyes fixed on distant stars, said nothing.

"Scrubbing it?" asked Cook. "But it's on the schedule. What do I tell the press?"

"That the President's not feeling well," said Strong. "Indigestion. Blame it on the kielbasa in Green Bay. We never get more than five percent of the Polish vote anyway."

SEGMENT
TWO

## STANTON SWEEPS WISCONSIN PRIMARY
### LAST-MINUTE KLECK BACKING
### FAILS TO HELP PRESIDENT

—*Headline,* Washington Post, May 17

# THE WHITE HOUSE WEST WING

## MAY 16 (9:00 A.M.)

★ Regis Strong got the news he'd been expecting before the sun rose over the Potomac. It was based on network wake-up surveys—sampling registered voters by phoning them at home instead of waiting till they exited the voting booths. As a TV innovation, it shaved ninety minutes off the time the networks needed to predict election results.

★ 53 ★

As a result, by 7:15 A.M. (8:15 in Washington) the networks had already confirmed a Stanton landslide, on a sampling of two percent of the state's early birds. This saved any late-rising Wisconsinites whatever time and energy they might have wasted going to the polls to vote in the primary. It also had Strong on the phone, telling me a White House staff car would be picking me up at my house at 8:30.

By 8:50, after being speed-whipped across Memorial Bridge through rush-hour traffic by one of the Handymen, I was deposited at the West Wing portico, then swept into the chief of staff's inner office.

Strong got straight to the point, before I even had a chance to balance my coffee cup.

*Excerpt of transcript, Tape 104-X, taped conversation between Regis Strong, WH chief of staff, and Frank Lee, VP press secretary, 16 May (0855 hours).*

RS: Stanton's getting eighty percent of the sampling that watched the debate, so it's all over in America's dairyland. Now everything comes down to what happens two weeks from today, Grits Tuesday.

FL: The Southern primaries—

RS: Right. Eleven states, Virginia to Texas. Tell me, Lee, what does your boss's schedule look like between now and then?

FL: I don't know offhand, I'd have to . . . why?

RS: Two weeks, that's all we need.

FL: You're not suggesting . . .

RS: *(Expletive deleted)*, what's the difference, seventy-two hours, fourteen days, it's all the same. I've already checked it out with Attorney General Kaufman, and he says—

FL: A two-week cover-up?

RS: Wrong. People cover up crimes, Lee, but what we have here, according to the AG, isn't a crime. No violation of the law, as far as he can see.

FL: Well, what is it? I mean—

RS: An exigency of state. That's what the AG calls it. You want to read his legal opinion? Here—

FL: A two-week exigency?

RS: So? Look, Lee, it's not as if we're doing anything original. Check your history. For all anybody knew, Woodrow Wilson was dead six months before his wife told anyone. Everybody does it. The Russians, hey—a limo drives into the Kremlin every morning, leaves every evening, nobody saw Andropov or Chernenko for three months. Who knew whether they were still around?

FL: But this isn't Russia. A two-week cover-up, exigency, whatever you call it—

RS: What are you worried about, Lee, the press? I thought the care and feeding of the media was your specialty. Fourteen days, that's all. The same plan we had for Wisconsin, except this time we get the votes.

FL: Same plan? You're going to promise eleven governors the Vice Presidential nomination?

RS: Actually only five or six; but that's not your load. All you have to do is keep the Vice President's office humming and work things out with the Second Lady.

FL: That's all? Look, there's an old Lincoln saying, "You can fool some of the people—"

RS: Lee, we're not talking about fooling all the people, because we don't have to. The polls show that eight percent of the American people could care less whether your boss is dead or alive because they don't even know we have a Vice President. But that's neither here nor there, because the operative saying in your case—to quote the AG—is "In for a penny, in for a ton." It's all there in his legal opinion. Read it over. Take your time. I don't have another appointment for, let's see, nine and a half minutes.

Understand, I don't have to level like this. There are other ways. I could tell you I was an innocent gone astray, a wide-eyed idealist misled by a cynical, corrupt crowd. Threatened, coerced, I lost my moral compass and was victimized by the System.

I could say that, but it would be pure bullshit.

Besides, as my PR mentor Phil Madvig always advises miscreant clients, "Confession is good for the image." So let me be candid: Strong had hit me where I was most vulnerable. Oh, I was still concerned about Bully's good name. And I still couldn't stomach the idea of Stanton sitting in the Oval Office. But something played a larger role.

It was simply this: blind flackery. Strong had it right. Dealing with the media—manipulation, smoke and mirrors—that's my specialty, my mission in life. Even an alter ego has an ego of his own. So I couldn't, never in a million election quadrennials, have resisted the supreme gambit. To shape Bully Vandercleve's image and cosmetize his foibles while he was alive had been a challenge. But to cover up his nonexistence for two entire weeks . . . *that* would be an exploit.

## GOLDBERG'S DELI

### MAY 16 (4:30 P.M.)

"I told you so."

In times of uncertainty it's reassuring to have friends like Sam Andreas, rocks of predictability who can be counted on to do and say the expected.

By late afternoon Tuesday, "Operation Avis," as Strong code-named our extended cover-up, was geared to go. I'd lined up three of the four people I thought were indispensable to keep the Vice President's image alive and well for fourteen more days.

The Second Lady had listened with a kind of clinical detachment, then said she knew I'd be calling as soon as she heard the results from Wisconsin. Interesting. I'd always had Cissy down as a political amateur—a petition bearer, a party giver—but never gave her credit for moxie. In politics, as old man Madvig used to say, you live and unlearn.

Still, moxie or no moxie, the question was, Would she cooperate? "Do I have a choice?" she replied. "In for a penny"—her exact words—"in for a ton."

I left the Vice President's residence with a clear impression that after years spent as a smiling backdrop for a philandering husband, Bully Vandercleve's bereaved wife didn't at all mind being a key player in a Presidential campaign.

Next on my list was McCluskey. The Vice President's chief of staff handled Bully's scheduling and appointments. An early-Mass Catholic, he had to be approached with a certain moral delicacy, so I opened and closed our session with a prayer for both Bully's immortal soul and temporal reputation.

McCluskey, the Boston teetotaler, listened, asked for a stiff pop—an abrupt conversion to Washington habit that would bear watching—but ended up agreeing there was no other choice: Bully would have wanted him to see the big picture.

Third, I visited Miriam Littlepaugh, the VP's personal secretary and the only staffer in position to see Bully actually enter and leave his EOB office every day. Loyal to a fault, Miriam was scared speechless that word might get out about the Vice President's last hours, not to mention shitless over the prospect of trying to survive in a world without Bully Vandercleve to keep her on retainer.

She listened, hyperventilated halfway through my spiel, but recovered and, like McCluskey, fell into line.

That left Sam. I'd saved what I knew would be my hardest sell for last. He didn't disappoint.

"Say it again, Sam."

"I told you so."

"Okay, you were right, I was wrong. But as you're fond of saying, that was then, this is now. The reason I need to talk to you is—"

"Forget it," he said. "No chance."

It was 4:30. Once again we were in a back room booth at Sam's preferred Jewish-Korean chophouse. This time he was sampling a snack of Mr. Kim-Goldberg's $3.25 house specialty, corned beef–and–kimchi pâté. I settled for a bottle of Dr. Brown's Cel-Ray Tonic.

"Sam, you don't even know what I want."

"Like hell I don't," he said spooning up a glob of kimchi. "You forget, I got sources. Fourteen days? I'll say it again, Lee: You're in over your head."

"Maybe," I said, "but I'm learning, fast. This time around I have a game plan," which I proceeded to detail, step by devious step: the Second Lady would continue to cover the Vice President's absence on the home front, using all the standard Washington excuses for avoiding or canceling out on social events, e.g., scheduling conflict, political obligations, national emergency, etc. Bully's status as a man of wealth and power gave him the social privilege of being where he wanted, when he wanted. The assumption about such men—i.e., "They wouldn't be there if they didn't know something"—precludes any suspicion they might not actually be there.

"Okay, you got the home front covered," said Sam, studying the glob of kimchi with growing suspicion. "But what about the staff?"

"That's where you come in," I replied.

The staff: There were eighty-odd vice presidential assistants on Capitol Hill and in the EOB, including secretaries, mail clerks, deputies, and deputies' deputies. Other than McCluskey, Littlepaugh, and me, few ever saw, much less had access, to their boss. Bully seldom went to the Hill, and when he did it wasn't to go to his Capitol office but only to sit beside our semicomatose Speaker of the House during the President's State of the Union speech, or to break a rare tie vote in the Senate.

As for the time spent in the EOB, the Vice President was transported each day from an opaque-glass limo through a rear office door to a fast-moving elevator. Give or take five seconds for the elevator door to open and close, the Secret Service had the movement down to a minute and a half—a human swirl in a musty government corridor, leaving in its wake a flotsam of low-level staffers to murmur "The Vice President"—though the man himself was only a blurred image engulfed by a mass of dark blue suits. And if the swirl didn't appear on a particular day? More presumptions. People would conclude that the Vice President had either come or gone earlier or later, that he was on a speaking trip, or out of the country at a state funeral.

"Bringing the Vice President to and from the residence every day," I said, winding down. "That's where I need you, Sam. Where the Vice President needs you."

Spoon still poised in midair, Sam shook his head. "I don't like it," he said. "Using the Service as part of a cover-up."

"An exigency of state," I corrected. "And I don't like it either. But if the Service won't do it, Strong plans to use the Handymen as a phony detail."

"I like that even less," Sam scowled. He finally took the plunge, burying the spoon in his mouth, then chewing slowly, carefully. "Those clowns passing themselves off as Secret Service could ruin the agency's reputation."

"My thought exactly."

He put down the spoon and studied his plate. "I think I'd been better off with the knockwurst," he said. I poured him a glass of Dr. Brown's. He sipped, swallowed, and set his jaw. "Okay," he said, shoving his plate aside. "I'll talk to the Director. We'll go along with the cover-up, but understand"—he shook a finger in my face—"it's not for you and not for that bastard Strong. It's for reputation—the Vice President's and the agency's."

"Fair enough," I said, and picked up the check, my attention now turned to the last, most slippery step of all—conning my way through the Vice President's schedule for the next two weeks.

**MEMORANDUM**

# OFFICE OF THE VICE PRESIDENT
## WASHINGTON

**DATE:** May 17
**FROM:** Martin A. McCluskey
**TO:** Frank Lee
**SUBJECT:** *Operation Avis*

Re our conference earlier this date, I have reviewed the Vice President's schedule commitments through May 30. Following are appointments and appearances penciled in for said period:

**May 18:** Otto De Faye. Haircut appointment canceled Monday, rescheduled this date/ 9:30–10:00 A.M.

**May 19:** Dr. Kissinger. Appointment canceled Friday, rescheduled this date/2:15–3:15 P.M.

**May 20:** Cabinet meeting. WH/10:00–11:00 A.M.

**May 21:** Reception and dinner, British embassy, honoring Lady Lambeth (nee Margaret Thatcher) former UK Prime Minister/7:00 P.M. (Formal)

**May 22:** TV interview with Ben Colfax/2:00– 2:45 P.M., CNN studios, M Street, N.W.

**May 26:** Commencement address, Barton Academy, Barton, Connecticut/10:00 A.M. (Overnight 5/25 at Sheraton Barton)

Also be advised that at the request of the WH, the VP is expected to place the traditional LD call to the winners' locker room following either the fourth, fifth, sixth, or seventh game of the National Basketball Association championship round. Approximate time frame: May 24–30.

In addition to the above, you should know that four incoming phone calls in the past twenty-four hours require the VP's personal attention: two (2) from Charles Foster Abel and two (2) from FBI Director Maximilian M. Mize.

Would appreciate your input on these matters ASAP.

McC.

## THE VICE PRESIDENT'S PRESS OFFICE
### MAY 17 (9:30 A.M.)

For a Vice President of the United States, the trick to being alive—so far as the public and news media are concerned—is either to make a gaffe or stir a controversy. There are no other ways. With Bully gone, my job was not only covering up in places he might be missed, but taking up the perceptual slack.

Unfortunately, Phil Madvig was still in London, fighting the PR "Battle of Buckingham," masterminding Prince Charles's clever move for a reconciliation (CHUCK TO DI: "LET'S MEND IT FOR THE TYKES' SAKE") It would have been reassuring to have my old mentor nearby, but it looked like exam time for Frankie; I was an alter ego flying solo.

Perusing McCluskey's memorandum, I saw targets of opportunity as well as high-risk areas. Some items on the VP's two-week schedule would be easy to blow away, e.g., De Faye the barber (or as he preferred, hairstylist) and Kissinger the global kibitzer (or as *he* preferred, *éminence grise*). They could be scrubbed with no pain (the good doctor might grouse, of course, but that was McCluskey's headache). Ditto the Cabinet meet. Bully hadn't attended one (or been missed at one) in more than a year.

As for the Lady Lambeth dinner, that was a White House hand-me-down—an event the President just didn't care to attend.

Looking for a Vice Presidential gaffe that might keep Bully "alive" in the news, I considered drafting an insensitive, sexist "Dear Maggie" letter of regret, then thought better of it. Bully was known to be insensitive and sexist at times, but never to an English peer. I opted for having McCluskey, as chief of staff, call the State Department. Not necessarily the Secretary of State (an airborne vagabond, seldom in this country), but the Brit desk. They'd have to find another surrogate for Hertz, because Avis had a sudden, unexpected schedule conflict.

Scrubbing the Barton commencement would be a bit more ticklish. Bully had a special place in his blue-blooded heart for his old prep school. But a call from McCluskey to the headmaster would do the job there, especially if it went through Signal. Long before, I'd learned that the words "the White House is calling" worked miracles in turning otherwise shrewd people to jelly.

That left the Colfax interview. Ben Colfax, the Prince of Darkness. When provoked, the Rambo of Washington columnists. *Nobody* ever scrubbed a TV guest appearance on the Bottoms-Colfax cable show—certainly not an interview locked in months before. A letter wouldn't do for this one. A phone call from McCluskey wouldn't do. I'd have to handle it myself, God help me.

Having worked out a PR strategy to cover the Vice President's inability to be where he was supposed to be the following two weeks, my next move was to defuse any random suspicion that he might not be anywhere at all. Even bad news, in this Vice President's case, was better than no news.

Ankle-deep in pending mail and news clips, I started searching for potential gaffes and controversies, the sort of items Americans expect to read and hear about Vice Presidents. For me, it was a clear 180. After a career spent stamping out PR brushfires, I'd signed on with the arsonists.

The search didn't take long. Ten minutes into the mail backlog, I ran into a questionnaire from *Ms.* magazine. Gloria Steinem was surveying U.S. public officials on issues from nuclear power to the 65-MPH speed limit. It was made to order for an insensitive, sexist, news-making reply, one part gaffe, one part controversy.

Next, there was an invitation from the S. J. Glick Memorial Sun Devil Golf Classic. That's the event where I'd screwed up the year before, letting Bully have his photo taken with "Miss Arizona Commerce."

Dear Mr. Vice President,

Last year you were kind enough to take time from your busy schedule to join us in our Sixth Annual Sun Devil Pro-Am Golf Classic. We trust that you enjoyed yourself, despite the unfortunate picture-taking incident that occurred in the clubhouse after the event. In that hope, we would again like to extend an invitation for you to take part in our Seventh Annual Classic, scheduled for September 23–26 at the Kush Country Club, Scottsdale, Arizona.

As in the past, all proceeds from the Classic will go to a worthy cause, my late father's (and the Classic founder's) favorite charity, the American Society of Cosmetic Surgery, which annually provides over $1 million in medical services to indigent young film and television performers.

With the sincere wish that bygones are bygones—and with extra precautions taken to bar unauthorized personnel from the clubhouse—we look forward to your being with us this coming September 23. Awaiting your response, I remain,

Very truly yours,

*Samuel J. Glick, Jr.*

SAMUEL J. GLICK, JR.
Classic Chairman

Old man Madvig had a rule—I forget the number—that once mangled, a client should never return to the scene of a PR accident. Not unless you want the media to rehash the episode; which, of course, was exactly what I had in mind.

Finally, I wanted an unmitigated controversy—some senseless imbroglio to establish, beyond any doubt, that the thin-skinned, media-bashing Bully Vandercleve the press knew during three presidential campaigns was still alive and bitching. Again, my search was brief. The item, from Ricky Hewlett's Q-and-A column in the May issue of *Washingtonian* magazine, fairly jumped off the page.

> Q.  What's this I keep hearing about Vice President Vandercleve's hippie daughter? Does she really work in a Baltimore strip joint as a topless singer? S.L., Takoma Park, Maryland.
>
> A:  There's been talk along that line, but at last report the Veep's daughter was doing her singing for a little-known rock group, The Heimlich Maneuver, which has yet to cut a profitable record. One reason may be that, as a lead vocalist, Connie Vandercleve gives a fair imitation of Kermit the Frog in full cry.

Perfect. Just what Operation Avis needed. Now, gaffes in one hand, controversies in the other, I could get down to business. Sticky business, because the time had come to bring my office inquisitor, Carla Braunschweig, into the loop.

## THE EOB AUTOPEN ROOM

### MAY 17 (11:30 A.M.)

For the record, the magic hand wasn't my first option. Only my first practical option. I would have preferred using Miriam Littlepaugh, Bully's DOF (Designated Office Forger), who handled the single-shot signatures when he was on the road, out of sorts, or otherwise unavailable to sign important letters.

But Miriam (like McCluskey) was something less than your ideal co-conspirator. She wasn't taking the heat too well, her talent for forgery only a quivering shadow of itself, which meant using the Autopen and adding Carla to the Need to Know list. She'd be a pain in the gluteus—as bad as Sam—but it was the price I had to pay for being a mechanical idiot: I needed her to move the magic hand.

It was a metallic gray box kept under lock and key on the third floor. About three feet wide and two feet deep—dressing table height. The one we used was prehistoric, a model out of the 1970s. In its time it had forged the signatures of a generation of Vice Presidents, from Fritz to Bully. It was steady, passionless, unflappable—like Carla when I broke the news to her about Operation Avis.

I was seated in my office, twirling my Greek worry beads (a souvenir relic from Bully's bacchanalian trip to Athens, after his second losing presidential campaign). She was standing to the right of my desk, just beneath a rear portrait of Hannibal Hamlin, Lincoln's first Vice President (dumped as part of the Republican Southern strategy in the campaign of 1864). She heard me out, looked at me, then through me. Then she crossed the room to stare out the window at the White House.

I twirled and waited. The inquiry was about to start. Carla never uttered a declarative sentence when a question would suffice.

"Through the Southern primaries?"

"Grits Tuesday," I said. "The next morning—"

"But suppose nothing is settled in the Southern primaries?"

I laughed. "Carla," I said, "you're a good friend and a great deputy press secretary. But as a political expert, you don't know squat."

Looking back, it wasn't just déjà vu, it was an omen. But as Julius Caesar once said, who digs omens nowadays?

Carla lifted the lid, then held up two brass objects with mysterious wavy edges. "Which signature do you want for the Glick letter?"

"Make it 'Bully,' " I said. "He knew Glick's old man pretty well."

She hitched one of the objects to a stylus held by thin silver strips, slid the first letter into place, and flipped the switch.

"How did Romana Clay take it when you told her about the two extra weeks?" she asked, as the moving stylus moved across the paper.

"Of all the members of the White House press corps, Romana Clay is the least of my worries," I replied. "For one thing, she won't be asking for any live interviews."

She cut the switch, then drew the letter out of the box.

## THE VICE PRESIDENT
### WASHINGTON

May 17

Mr. Samuel J. Glick, Jr.
The S. J. Glick Memorial Sun Devil Golf Classic
6529 Kush Drive
Scottsdale, Arizona 24784

Dear Sam:

I was delighted to receive your letter inviting me to take part in this year's Seventh Annual Sun Devil Golf Classic. You are quite correct in believing that I had a marvelous time at last year's Classic, clubhouse incidents to the contrary notwithstanding.

Barring the unforeseen, you'll see me on September 23, ready to tee off. Someone from my advance staff will be in touch with your office shortly.

Very truly yours,

STEWART B. VANDERCLEVE

"And it came to pass," I said, "that I beheld the wonders of modern technology. Man's handiwork. Perfect, Carla, perfect."

"Reloading," she replied, slipping the second letter into place. "Are you sure about this one?"

"Not only sure, I want it hand delivered to Hewlett this afternoon."

"You're off the scope," she said, her first declarative sentence of the morning. "Either that or a genius."

Actually, as I look back on it, a little of each. Off the scope for going that far with Operation Avis, a genius in the way I was carrying it out.

"Which sig this time?" Carla wanted to know.

"Stiff and formal," I replied. " 'Stewart B. Vandercleve,' with a flourish."

"The Autopen doesn't do flourishes," she replied. "You'll have to settle for stiff. Appropriate, wouldn't you say?"

She flipped the switch.

"McCluskey called again," she said as the machine clicked off. "Poor fella's having a nervous breakdown. Will he make it through the next two weeks?"

I shrugged, as if the question were irrelevant (though it had also passed through my mind). Carla slid the letter off the tray and handed it to me, at arm's length, as if it were a king rattler.

## OFFICE OF THE VICE PRESIDENT

### WASHINGTON

May 17

Mr. Richard Hewlett
Columnist
*Washingtonian* Magazine
1828 L Street, N.W.
Washington, D.C. 20036

Dear Sir:

Your insulting column comparing my daughter's singing talent to that of Kermit the Frog has been brought to my attention. This is to advise, both personally and officially, that if by any unfortunate chance we ever have occasion to meet, you may end up needing not only a beefsteak for your critical eye but an industrial strength truss.

Sincerely,

STEWART B. VANDERCLEVE

It was straight out of Harry Truman's book, but any old controversy will do in a storm.

Next came my pièce de résistance: Vice President Vandercleve's reply to the *Ms.* magazine questionnaire.

"The formal sig for this one, right?"

"Certainly not," I replied. "For Steinem, make it 'Bully.' She'll take it as patronizing."

Carla shook her head. "No question about it," she said. "You're off the scope." She hesitated a moment, then put the magic hand into play. . . .

# THE VICE PRESIDENT
## WASHINGTON

May 17

Miss Gloria Steinem
Editoress Emerita
*MS.*
119 West 40th Street
New York, NY 10018

Dear Glo:

Sorry not to have replied to your questionnaire earlier, but I'm sure you'll understand the hectic life we lead in this man's world of government and politics. I wish I could take the time to reply to your questions, but frankly, I can't see much point in it. The issues you ask about are of a serious variety that I doubt most of your readers are interested in.

Far be it from me to tell you how to run your magazine, but wouldn't you fare better by sticking to household hints and recipes? Along that line, I am sending along a recipe for blueberry muffins, taken from the *Capitol Hill Wives' Country Cookbook.* It's one of my favorites.

Sincerely,

STEWART B. VANDERCLEVE

Like dominoes falling:

★ Glick cranked out a press release the same day he received Bully's acceptance letter. Reaction in Washington was just what I'd hoped for.

Excerpt, *Newsweek* magazine "Periscope" column:

That Dilettante Veep is back, as fun-loving as ever. It was only last September that Vice President Vander-cleve landed prat-first in the nation's supermarket tabloids after an embarrassing photo session at a celebrity golf tournament out West. Now, baffling not only the political pundits but his own advisers, the VP has decided to thumb his nose at the "Dump Bully" wing of the GOP by accepting an invitation to take part in the same tournament come September, reviving old questions not only about his personal life-style but his judgment. . . .

★ *Washingtonian* magazine had copies of the letter to Rickie Hewlett on the street within thirty minutes after it was hand delivered. The wire services moved a blown-up repro, Bully's signature prominent, across the country. In an interview on "Entertainment Tonight," Hewlett said that while he wasn't intimidated by the VP's threats, the letter was "certain to have a chilling effect on rock music critics across America." *USA Today* ran the story beneath a Page One headline:

### VEEP TO
### DAUGHTER'S CRITICS:
### "DROP DEAD"

★ Steinem was on five TV talk shows, including "Good Morning, America," "Today," and the "CBS Morning News"; Oprah Winfrey's producer, then Winfrey herself, called the press office to ask whether the Vice President would appear on her show, either to debate Steinem or otherwise talk about his views on the modern American woman. Phil Donahue topped her offer. If necessary, said Donahue, he'd move his staff and production crew to Washington for a day to do the interview.

But again, there were omens. The National Sharpshooters Association gave the Vice President its "Bull's-Eye of the Week" award for "hitting the mark in speaking out for traditional American values," while Cissy Vandercleve, of all people, reached me on a secured White House line to ask what the hell I was trying to do to her husband's political image? Turn him into a Right-wing troglodyte?

I'd put in the call after delaying it as long as possible. Now, however, after listening to the Prince bellow for the better part of the morning, a light slowly began to dawn. Madvig's Rule Number 5: *When a client hands you a lemon, why stop with a lemonade? Make it into a Tom Collins.*

So Ben Colfax was piqued. Fine. Maybe his pique could be turned to advantage. He liked "dump" stories? Give him a "dump" story. A Tom Collins of a "dump" story.

"The reason he won't go on, Ben—" I began.

"Yeah?"

"The reason—I didn't intend to tell you, but we really owe you one. The reason is—"

"I'm listening."

"It's that the Vice President is afraid he might say something that would tick off the President. Things, you know, are up in the air right now."

Sudden, blessed silence on the other end.

"Ben? Are you still there?"

"What do you mean, up in the air?"

"Well, anything can happen, you know? He was telling me just this morning that the White House is looking for the slightest excuse to bump him from the ticket."

More blessed silence.

Then: "Who's 'he'? Are you talking about Vandercleve? *He*

★ 71 ★

told you that? Let's get the ground rules straight, Lee. Is this off the record or for attribution?"

I clucked my tongue, stirring in the gin. "Any way you want it, Ben," I said. "Any way you want it."

Jackpot. The Vice President had just given his first posthumous interview.

# 5

VANDERCLEVE SEES WHITE HOUSE
PLOT TO DUMP HIM

by "Foggy" Bottoms and Ben Colfax

*—from the* Washington Post
*Op-Ed page, May 21*

## THE PRESS SECRETARY'S FAMILY ROOM

MAY 21 (8:30 A.M.)

★ "Come on, admit it. You haven't even *looked* at the thing."

"What? Oh, sorry, son. You were saying?"

"Saying, you haven't even . . . Oh, to hell with it. Just forget I ever asked."

★ 73 ★

*To hell with it?* That brought me around, all right. Precocious brat, sassing his father during Quality Time at the breakfast table; though in fairness, the kid did have a point: my attention was elsewhere, still focused on my traditional early morning call.

The caller this Sunday wasn't Romie Clay but McCluskey, all wrought up over the Bottoms-Colfax column. Where, he wanted to know, had they been able to contact the Vice President? Was I *positive* Bully was dead? Maybe there'd been a mix-up. Maybe this was all a bad dream, the boss was still alive, and . . .

I reassured him (if that's the appropriate verb) that Bully was indeed dead and the column had been planted; at which point he broke down, blubbering, "I'm headed to Mass to ask divine guidance."

*Divine guidance?* Good God! Did that mean Confession? If so, was McCluskey's family priest a discreet Republican or a garrulous Democrat? Clearly, a touch of Sam Andreas's Potomac paranoia had rubbed off on me, but considering the delicate balance of McCluskey's psyche, I didn't let on. The way we left it, he promised to cap his emotions for twenty-four hours, say an extra Our Father for me, and drop by the press office first thing Monday.

But Mac's call wasn't the only disturbing news to reach me that Sunday morning. There was also bad news in the sports section. Not the Mets-Cardinal game—they'd been rained out—but the inexorable progress of the NBA title series. The Sonics had won the night before, putting them one game up on the Knicks. I needed a long series, six or seven games, to give me time to finesse Bully's scheduled call-in to the winning coach.

Scrubbing the call-in was always possible, but dangerous. Nothing is more likely to arouse suspicion over the state of an American politician's health than if he skips out on featured billing at a sports event.

It was a hand-me-down event, one the President could care less about. That was one of the administration's best-kept secrets: for the first time since Coolidge, the United States had someone in the Oval Office who neither knew nor cared anything about spectator sports.

Early on, Regis Strong and the White House PR team had tried to paper over this character flaw by persuading the President—

against his better judgment—to put in a locker-room call to Mike Ditka, coach of the Chicago Bears, after Ditka's second Super Bowl win. The conversation, telecast nationally, had been the worst presidential PR disaster since Jimmy Carter tried to run a six-miler. Not only did Hertz mispronounce Ditka's name ("Good to talk to you, Spike"), but referred to the Bears' having won "the Super Goal"; worse yet, he signed off hoping "Spike" and the Bears would win the NFL title "next season and for many seasons to come," thereby locking up the Chicago vote and alienating fans in two dozen other NFL cities.

After that debacle, Strong passed all sports events on to the Vice President—from locker room call-ins to throwing out the first ball of the baseball season. It was one of the few ceremonial functions of his Vice Presidency that Bully enjoyed, and he did it well, that is, gaffelessly.

But now what? Since Bully couldn't make the call to the winning NBA coach, we'd have to take our chances with the President. The lesser of two risks. That was our only option, unless, of course, Strong had some bigger picture in mind, which, it figured, he would.

"You really should take time to read the speech," Mo was saying, as we crammed soiled Melmac into the dishwasher. "The boy looks up to you, Frank. He worships the ground his father walks on."

*Guilt.* Some feel it, others pass it on. Among the items of contention that drove my bleeding-heart spouse and me into the arms of an upscale $150-per-hour marriage counselor was her ability to do the latter, in large dollops. Did the boy *really* worship the ground his father walked on? Only if there was something going on sixteen years ago between his mother and Che Guevera or Bruce Springsteen, the only subjects our son ever mentioned in idolatrous terms.

Still, her point was well taken. I'd been derelict in not having read over Tommy's first cut at a valedictory speech for his high school graduation. Dishwashing chores complete, I entered my den, turned on the ball game (sound down), settled back and began reading. I got no further than the title—"Arise, Young America!"—

when, worst luck, with two on, two down, and Kevin McReynolds batting, the phone rang.

Romie Clay, of course.

*Transcript, Tape No. 217-B, telephone conversation between Frank Lee, press secretary to the Vice President, and Romana Clay, 21 May (1315 hours).*

FL:   *(Expletive deleted)* third strike!

RC:   Lee? I'm calling from Birmingham.

FL:   Oh—Romie? Yeah, I—uh—caught you on the tube last night. You're covering Stanton this week, right?

RC:   Stanton this week, then the President's campaign till Grits Tuesday. You sitting down?

FL:   Yeah, why?

RC:   I just interviewed Stanton. He says he's got the bull by the horns.

FL:   Bull?

RC:   As in "market." The day after Grits Tuesday, he plans to reopen hearings on insider trading, and his first witness will be—

FL:   Don't tell me. C. Foster Abel?

RC:   The same. Executor, he says, of the Vice President's blind trust. Is that right?

FL:   Right, but—

RC:   Then, with the cameras off, he tells me, for attribution to a "highly placed committee source," who'll be subpoenaed after Abel. One guess.

FL:   The joke's on him. Day after Grits Tuesday there won't be any One Guess to subpoena. We're making the announcement before—

RC:   Yeah, that's what you told me last week, remember?

## VANDERCLEVE STRATEGY HAS EXPERTS STUMPED

*—Headline, page 2,*
Washington Post, May 22

It was one of those stories known as thumb suckers: one-fifth news, four-fifths random quotes from various has-beens, never-beens, and campaign kibitzers who make up the Washington Experts pool.

"What is 'Bully' Vandercleve up to?" the piece began. "Not since Spiro Agnew has a sitting Vice President taken to media bashing with the reckless abandon Vandercleve showed last week in assailing the editor of the nation's leading women's magazine and a widely read gossip columnist . . ."

Good, and it got even better. The theory that Bully's week of controversy was some subtle "strategy" to box the President into keeping him on the ticket was the sage contribution of Josh Ward, an itinerant Democratic pollster whose claim to expertise rested on his having masterminded Walter Mondale's sweep of Minnesota and the District of Columbia in the presidential campaign of 1984. It made for a harebrained but delicious read, evidence that our real strategy had worked. We could coast from now till Grits Tuesday. Operation Avis, after little more than a week, had taken on a life of its own.

## AIR FORCE ONE, DESCENDING ON SHREVEPORT

### MAY 22 (11:00 A.M.)

*The President was livid. Holding clips of Sunday's Bottoms-Colfax column in one hand and the* Post's *"strategy" story in the other, he fixed his chief of staff with a laser gaze, half-fire, half-ice.*

*"What is this crud?" he rasped; then, once more with feel-*

ing, "What is this crud? *Vandercleve here, Vandercleve there, on the morning news, the evening news, that's all I read and hear. And you tell me the man won't hold a press conference to announce—"*

"His press secretary says—"

"Let me finish! *I said, the sonofabitch won't follow orders and announce his withdrawal, won't even, according to my own chief of staff, accept an invitation to discuss the matter with his* President! *Here I am, on the road, busting my regal ass, trying to save my party, my country, the Free World. And what support do I get from my own Vice President? From my own* staff? *Nada, zero,* zip!"

"Mr. President, *these partition walls are fairly thin and we've got guests coming on board—"*

"I haven't *finished!" said the President, now crumpling the news clips and propelling them across the cabin. "Something is going on, Regis, and I, dammit, pay your salary to know about these things. How in Christ's name am I supposed to convince the Governor of Florida, the Governor of Texas, the Governor of Louisiana—"*

"Who's *coming on board, sir, any second—"*

"How am I *supposed to convince* any *governor that he alone is my choice for Vice President when all we read about is the man I'm supposed to be* dumping? *Tell me, Mr. Strong,* how?"

"Something snapped in Vandercleve just after that break-fast," said Strong. "Allergy, trauma, midlife crisis, who knows? But the plan's working anyway." *He pointed to a computer printout on the cabin desk. "The tracking polls look good, the endorsements are coming through—"*

"Horseshit!" *said the President. "I want—now listen care-fully, the only President we have is telling you what he wants—I want to* talk *to Vandercleve. Breakfast, lunch, coffee break, in the Cabinet Room urinal. Want to* talk *to Mr. High-and-Mighty when we get back to Washington, to give him his marching—"*

*The President, face suddenly flushed, sat down.*

"Do you need Doc Berger?" *asked Strong.*

*The President shook his head.*

*"Water?"*

*The President nodded. Strong filled a paper cup and handed it to his chief. The President drained the cup, then jerked his head toward the desk phone, and said, "Get him on the line."*

*"Who?" asked Strong.*

*"Who?" The President crushed the paper cup and threw it to the cabin floor. "Jesse Jackson, that's* who! *The mayor of Shreveport! Who the hell have I been talking about, Mr. Strong? Get that miserable two-faced Vice President of mine on the line. Now!"*

*"Now?" said Strong. "Look, we land in fifteen minutes. On the ground you'll have a secured line. But an airborne call is radio, the whole world can listen—"*

*"I don't give an expletive* who's *listening," said the President. "I said,* now!"

*Strong took a deep breath, pursed his lips, and headed for the plane's communications center. He scrawled a number on back of an Air Force One weather summary and handed it to the sergeant in charge. "Ask for the Vice President," he said. "I'll take the call in the President's cabin."*

*Transcript, Tape 105-L. Telephone conversation between Regis Strong, WH chief of staff, and Unidentified Second Party, 22 May (1115 hours).*

RS:   Hello? The Vice President's office? Regis Strong here, calling for the President.

USP:  Strong? What's up? I can hardly hear you.

RS:   That's right, the President wants to speak to the Vice President. Put him on the line. I'll hold.

USP:  What are you . . .

RS:   No, not—is that you, McCluskey? What's with your secretary, doesn't she understand English? I said I'm calling for the President. He wants to talk to your boss. Not you, but your boss.

USP: My boss? Oh—someone's in the room with you, right?

RS: You're *(expletive deleted)* well right. I said, Vice President Vandercleve and nobody else. Get him on the—no, no, I can handle it, Mr. President. Believe me, I can handle—

USP: Strong, are you—

P: This is the President. I want to—hello? Hello there? Well, I'll be a *(expletive deleted)*. The *(expletive deleted)* hung up in my face.


## THE VICE PRESIDENT'S PRESS OFFICE

### MAY 22 (NOON)


Maybe Sam was right: I was in over my head. Chutzpah, yes, but until Operation Avis I hadn't considered hanging up on presidents as part of my work ethic. On the other hand, why should I feel guilty? Frank Lee hadn't hung up on the Leader of the Free World, McCluskey had; at least, the President *thought* it was McCluskey, which was enough to cover my ass.

So much for guilt pangs. A demanding presence and the tantalizing scent of Elizabeth Taylor's Passion II brought things back into focus. It was Carla. "McCluskey's waiting to see you," she said. Then, leaning in to whisper: "I thought he was a teetotaler."

"He is," I replied. "Only drinks Diet Pepsi."

"Diet Pepsi," she snickered. "Sugar-free and eighty-six proof."

For once she was wrong. It was 100-proof Wild Turkey. McCluskey slouched into the room like a Gaelic wraith, the perfect figure of a world-weary Boston pol in decline.

"Diet Pepsi?" I asked, reaching across the desk to push the intercom buzzer.

He nodded yes; then, when Carla arrived at the door, mumbled, "Diet Pepsi."

"Two Diet Pepsis, Carla," I said, then turned back to McCluskey. He was holding a file folder with two shaky hands.

"Sorry I'm late," he said, "but I was held up."

"Understandable," I replied. "You're a busy man."

"No, I mean held up," he said, "as in robbed. Fifty dollars taken from me in Lafayette Square, right across from the White House. Two ruffians carrying placards at six-thirty this morning."

"Early," I said.

"I couldn't sleep, you know?"

"Did you report it to the police?"

"Got their descriptions, reported it to the police," he said. "That's why I'm late. They caught both of 'em, right there in the square. Hadn't budged from the spot where it happened." He tugged at his tie, a wide-bottomed orange-yellow, circa 1977. *"Their* story was that I hadn't been robbed but made a voluntary contribution to their cause."

"Novel defense," I said.

"But the cops believed it!" He shook his head. "Can you imagine? Their placards, Frank, were in Aramaic. They hardly spoke English. How could I *possibly* have made a fifty-dollar contribution to their cause?"

"Sometimes the system breaks down, Mac," I replied sympathetically. "It just breaks down. Speaking of which"—my eyes homed in on his file folder—"tell me about those problems that keep you awake at night."

He gazed down at the folder. "I don't know where to begin," he said. "Calls, correspondence, how do you want it? In ascending or descending order of importance?"

"Let's start at the bottom," I said. "Clear out the underbrush."

He grunted, opened the folder, and began thumbing through his notes. "Ascending, I would say Otto De Faye is less of a headache than Royce Percival, C. Foster Abel, or the director of the FBI. Then again, he's more insistent. Phones six times a day to say the Vice President is overdue for his regular weekly haircut. Or as he calls it, *sty-a-ling.* He's affected, you know.''

"So I've heard," I said. "Also, that he has a pretty active mouth to go with his big-name clientele. What have you told him?''

"Actually, after the second call, I turned him over to Miriam," said McCluskey, producing a handkerchief to dab at his forehead. "As I said yesterday, Frank, I'm not too good at this sort of thing.''

"'Um-hm," I said, getting up to come around the desk. "And what did Miriam tell him?''

"That the Vice President was tied up and we'd get back as soon as he had time for a sty-a-ling.''

"Why didn't she just say the Vice President's changed sty-a-lists?'' I asked.

McCluskey looked at me incredulously. "You obviously don't know Otto De Faye," he said. "Tell the Hairstylist of Presidents that he's lost a customer? He'd be here in ten minutes demanding to see the boss. He carries a White House pass, with perks. Goes all the way back to the Ford administration.''

"Only eight more days," I said. "Tell Miriam to hold the fort. Now what about Percival? You did scrub the Barton speech, didn't you?''

"Called him through Signal, just like you said. Didn't faze him. He insists his good friend the Vice President wouldn't cancel a commencement speech at his old school on such short notice. He blames it on the staff. A nasty fellow beneath the phony Yorkshire accent, Frank, really nasty.''

"Well, nasty or nice, he'll have to live with it.''

"But he won't, Frank. He's contacted everybody Bully went to Barton with, and they've called me—'' Now the folder began rattling, shedding its contents on the floor. Perched on the desktop, I reached over to steady him.

"Unwind, Mac," I said. "If it makes you feel any better, I'll take care of Otto De Faye and Percival.''

"And Abel and the director?''

"And Abel and the director." I waited a beat. Then: "What did Mize want? Did he say?''

"To speak to the Vice President, that's all I know. It's a matter, he says, of penultimate urgency and cardinal import. You know how he talks. Events necessitate, he said, an expeditious audience, forthwith, no caveats. His exact words, as Miriam took them down."

"But no idea what he has in mind?"

"Frank, I don't understand what the man says, much less what he means," said McCluskey, eyes clouding up. "The whole thing is just . . ."

Carla reentered the room, holding a tray bearing Diet Pepsis and plastic glasses. "Your son just called," she said, plunking the glasses onto the desktop. "I told him you'd call back." She unceremoniously handed McCluskey and me our colas, then turned to leave. "Anything else, your excellency? Perchance hors d'oeuvres?"

I had no idea why she was ticked—that's the way it goes with Method deputies—but I let her impudence pass, opting to concentrate on the problem posed by our co-conspirator's imminent nervous breakdown. Sweat ran from his receding red hairline, tears from his myopic red eyes.

"Mac," I said unctuously, drawing his can of Diet Pepsi from quivering fingers and pouring it into a glass. "We can't let the Vice President down now, can we? The three of us—you, Miriam, and me—for one brief shining moment, we were blessed. Privileged to work for one of nature's noblemen."

"That we were," McCluskey blubbered. "The Vice President was good to us, he was."

"And still can be," I said, pressing the case, eye to bloodshot eye. "Are you listening, Mac? Because what I have to say is very important to the Vice President, your family, and your golden years."

"Listening," he said tonelessly, holding the cold glass to his forehead.

"You have a lovely wife in Louise," I said.

"Lois," he corrected.

"And four wonderful kids."

"Six. Four boys, two girls."

"And a new summer beach home in Ocean City."

"A cottage in Hilton Head."

"With a mortgage hanging."

"You've got that part right." he said. "Not to mention college tuition. And to think, counting my military time, I only needed three years to qualify for federal retirement."

"Exactly," I said, switching gears from unctuous concern to hard salesmanship. "A mortgage, tuition, and only three years to lock up a richly deserved pension." I chucked him under the chin. "But listen to me, Mac, you don't have to sweat it. The Good Lord's still looking out for you and yours. If the President is re-elected—reelected with the help *you're* giving him—you'll still have a job, probably with a raise in supergrade, right here in the White House–EOB complex. For four more years."

I held up four fingers.

"You think so?" he asked plaintively. "You really think so?"

"Positive. Maybe not for the new VP, but a cushy job some-place around here."

He took a sip of cola and heaved a sigh. "When I woke up this morning," he said, not looking at me but at some mystic specter beyond my shoulder, "I knew I had to talk to someone, to let it all out. I'm glad now that I followed my own instinct instead of Lois's. She wanted me to talk to—"

"Lois knows about the Vice President?"

His puffed eyes widened to let me know I had just asked a remarkably obtuse question. "Lois and I have no secrets, Frank," he replied. "In twenty-eight years of marriage—"

"Who'd Lois want you to talk to?"

"Why, Father Teeley at St. Ignatius, of course," he replied. "Our parish priest."

"Of course," I said exhaling. My phone intercom buzzed.

"Your son's on the line again," Carla informed me. "He sounds irritated."

"Tell Tommy I'll be right with him," I said. I hung up the phone, lifted McCluskey from his chair, and led him toward the door. "Feeling better, Mac?" I said, summoning my last reserve of bonhomie for the day. "You go home now and get some sleep. Tell Lois that your instinct was right, there was no need to trouble Father Teeley with our petty office problems. You're lucky to have a wife like that—loyal, discreet. She *is* discreet, isn't she, Mac?"

"My Lois," he replied, holding out his hand as we stood by the door, "is as discreet as I am."

"That's reassuring," I said, taking his hand in both of mine. "God bless."

He wandered down the EOB corridor toward his office.

"Add Lois McCluskey to the list," I said to no one in particular.

"Add what?" asked Carla.

"Nothing," I replied. "Get my son on the line."

*Transcript, Tape No. 114-X, telephone conversation between Frank Lee, VP press secretary, and son, Thomas Lee, 22 May (1110 hours).*

TL: Frank? Mo told me to call. She said—

FL: Tommy, this is your father, and the person you refer to as "Mo" is your mother.

TL: Hey, do we have to go through that again?

FL: We'll go through it as many times—

TL: Okay, for the record: I know you're my father, you know you're my father. So why do we have to inhibit a meaningful relationship with the stricture of neobourgeois formalism?

FL: Because I happen to be a neobourgeois formalist, whatever that is, and I prefer that my sixteen-year-old son call me "Father," "Dad," or even "Pop." There is a fine line, Tommy, between—

TL: All right, Pop, we'll do it your way—for now. Your wife, my mother, a.k.a. "Mo," told me to call because it seems to have slipped your paternal mind that my graduation ceremony is a week from this coming Thursday, and I'm still looking for feedback on my valedictory speech.

★ 85 ★

FL: Oh, right, your valedictory speech. By the way, son, congratulations. Your mother and I are proud of you, very proud of you.

TL: Right. Now about the speech?

FL: The speech.

TL: You still haven't looked at it. Fine, I'll tell Mom—

FL: Don't jump to conclusions, Tommy. As a matter of fact, I have looked it over. Only a first read, but enough to give me a feel.

TL: And?

FL: I—uh—it's extremely relevant. A relevant speech, some nice turns of phrase—

TL: But?

FL: No buts, I liked it. I only wish the Vice President could get quality writing like that from his own speechwriters.

TL: Oh? You're just saying that—

FL: No. Really. And—uh—as I say, it's fine-tuned to the audience.

TL: You mean the graduating class. Well, yeah, it's pitched that way, for young people, but I don't know how the faculty will take it. Or the parents, you know?

FL: Faculty, parents—I see your point. Maybe, maybe the thing for me to do is look it over again, with that in mind.

TL: What about the Proudhon quote? Did I overdo it, going with the original French text? I wondered about that—"*Qu'est-ce que la proprieté? C'est le vol.*" Which do you think plays better, the original or a translation?

FL: Since you mention it, I'd go with a translation.

TL: What you've always preached, never overestimate the intelligence of a constituency, right?

FL: Exactly. What I've always preached. Listen, son, I hate to break this off, but the Vice President's calling. I'll get back to you.

TL: Right. So when can I expect—

FL: Tonight, tomorrow night, we'll get together and put the final touches on it. Okay?

TL: Okay, Pop.


Reenter Carla, bearing phone messages. While I was talking to Tommy, the Second Lady had called:

OFFICE OF THE VICE PRESIDENT

WASHINGTON, D.C.


*FL :*

*Mrs. V. wants to see you re Barton speech. ASAP.*

*CB*

*5/22*
*1 p.m.*


Lunch would be the Press Secretary's Blue Plate: a month-old Snyder's pretzel washed down with the lukewarm remnants of my Diet Pepsi, ingested on the run. I hailed a Yellow cab near Lafayette Square, an area congested with burnoosed protesters bearing indecipherable placards and chanting (as best I could hear over my

cabbie's xenophobic maledictions against foreign protesters),
"U.S. OUT OF KUMQUAT!"

It was the first of two traffic locks we encountered en route
to the Vice President's residence, spring being Washington's prime
season for protest rallies and filmmaking. The second, at Dupont
Circle, featured an ugly brood of leather-jacketed skinheads
harassing a busload of senior citizens, all under the approving eye
of a cordon of police. A shoot, my voluble cabbie informed me
(after muttered imprecations against "Hollywood big shots"), for
Brian DePalma's much-anticipated remake of *Mr. Smith Goes to
Washington.*

Once past Dupont Circle, however, it was clear driving up
Mass. Avenue to the Naval Observatory, where we hung a left,
were cleared at the entrance, and headed past the Secret Service
barriers to the residence gate.

"You work for Vandercleve?" the cabbie asked, counting out
my change.

"So they say," I replied noncommittally, handing back a lavish
Republican tip and girding for a diatribe against permissive immi-
gration laws and/or Hollywood big shots.

"Yeah, well tell him that, frankly, I never thought much of him
until he blasted that sumbitch critic who cut down his daughter.
Took real guts." He handed me a card.

E. RAY LARGE
CAB-LIMOUSINE SERVICE
DAY-R-NITE

Hackers Local 478          Phone 202/555-7713
*"America—Love It or Shove It"*

"Anything my friends and I can do for your boss, lemme
know."

"I'll keep that in mind," I said, one foot on the driveway.

"Will he be dumped?"

I smiled and thanked him for taking the scenic route.

"TELL HIM, HANG TOUGH!" he boomed, as I headed up the
veranda steps.

Amazing. It seemed that Bully dead was more popular than Bully living.

Astride her Schwinn Air-Dyne, the load indicator pushed to the max, Cissy Vandercleve was working off steam. The Second Lady, in a sweat, wore a green-and-white leotard (Adolfo) and green shoes (Reebok), topped by a white headband bearing the Vice Presidential seal. We were upstairs in what, the last time I was there, had been Bully's private den, newly renovated into a work-out room. Wall mementoes of the Vice President's career had been replaced by four-color LeRoy Nieman sketches of Babe Zaharias tee-ing off, Althea Gibson serving, and Mary Decker Slaney in full stride.

"Royce Percival is out of control," she huffed as I took a seat on a Nautilus workbench. "That pompous ass has phoned three times in the last twenty-four hours, asking for Bully. He says the office staff is hiding something. I agreed, of course."

"Yeah, well—you *agreed?*"

"Certainly. I told him I hadn't seen my husband in days, that the staff tells me he's tied up on some national security matter."

"You told him *what?*"

"Look, Frank, somebody's got to be the fall person if this plot of yours falls through, and it damned well won't be the grieving widow," she said, shifting from pedal to handlebar control. "Percival claims his friend the Vice President wouldn't have left him without a speaker this close to commencement. He has a point, you know?"

There was something different in her tone—a new imperialism, maybe just an aerobic high—that warned me to back off. "I'll buy that," I said agreeably. "But with Grits Tuesday only eight days away—"

"Stop kidding yourself, Frank," she said. "The tracking polls [Tracking polls? I had no idea she followed tracking polls] say, as of this morning, that Grits Tuesday won't settle anything. Stanton is ahead in six states, the President in seven. So"—she took a deep breath and shifted back to the pedals—"we wake up the morning after, four weeks till the convention, and what do you think Strong's line will be?"

I let the question float.

"In for a pound, in for a ton, that's what he'll say. All the way to L.A. That's where the convention is, right?"

"Anaheim," I replied. Then, finding the tenor of our colloquy depressing: "Getting back to Percival, any suggestions?"

The Air-Dyne peeper signaled the end of her thirty-minute ride. She slipped off the bike seat, then indicated (with an imperial gesture) that I was in the wrong place at the wrong time. I got up and out of the way, while she straddled the bench and commenced bicep flexing.

"I think—*uh*—the only way we can deal with Percival—*uh*—is to get him a speaker, a substitute, a—*uh*—what do you call it?"

"Surrogate?" I said. "Not a bad idea. Who do you have in mind?

As if I didn't know by then.

"Well, it so happens—*uh*—I'm not doing a thing on the thirtieth. Free as a bird."

"Oh?"

"And it's not —*uh*—as if I don't have surrogate experience. I've filled in for Bully before, remember?"

Indeed I did; the Cajun-American Political Action Committee in Eunice, Louisiana, where she endorsed ERA (which the administration opposed) and self-determination for Acadia (which the State Department had to look up on a map before issuing a "no comment").

"Possible," I replied, eyeing the sweat-soaked Vice Presidential seal on her imperial headband. "But I'll have to, you know, check it out."

"You do that," she said, finishing her reps. "Check it out and let me know." She began toweling off. "And Frank," she said, "if I do go, don't worry about a text. I'll write my own."


*Transcript, Tape 108-X, telephone conversation through Signal between Regis Strong, WH chief of staff, and Frank Lee, press secretary to the Vice President, 22 May (2115 hours).*

SIGNAL: Mr. Lee? Mr. Strong's on the line, from Atlanta.

FL: Good, I need to—

RS: Lee? Been trying to reach you. Hectic campaign day, five states, eight cities.

FL: Yeah, well, I've been busy, too. We've got problems, beginning with your phone call this morning. Can we talk or—

RS: The President's turned in, I'm alone, the line's secured. About the call, he wants to talk to your boss, you know?

FL: He wants to talk to my boss? Are you telling me Hertz isn't in the loop?

RS: It's, uh, an incidental I meant to tell you about but didn't get around to.

FL: Wait a minute—the man's President of the United States, his Vice President's dead. It seems to me he's entitled—

RS: It's the system, Lee, the way it works. The Presidency is too big for any one man so he delegates, and right now I'm the head delegee.

FL: Well, I don't know. (Inaudible) didn't buy into—

RS: Get with the program, Lee. You're supposed to be a pro, remember? Politics is made up of two kinds of people— those who want to run the country and those who'll settle for being President. I know what Hertz wants, I know what he needs. He wants four more years, he needs somebody around who sees the big picture.

FL: Yeah, but—

RS: No *(expletive deleted)* buts. Lee, I've got a President on my hands whose systolic numbers go off the chart when a report comes in over one page long. Short temper, short attention span. Next time, believe me, I'll get a younger candidate.

★ 91 ★

FL:     Hertz has high blood—

RS:     The operative word is pressure. It's the one thing, aside from microeconomics and negotiating with the Russians, he can't cope with. Other than that, he's a great candidate. So if I tell him Vandercleve's dead, we can kiss the nomination off. Not to mention my job. I'll be back writing ad copy for Whammo-Burgers. No way, friend, no way.

FL:     *(Inaudible)*

RS:     The bottom line? Okay, after Grits Tuesday, with the pressure off, we tell him his Vice President is dead and it'll make his day. But not until then—wait, somebody's at the door. Call you later.

## PRESIDENTIAL SUITE, ATLANTA OMNI

### MAY 22 (9:30 P.M.)

*"The boss wants to see you," said Simpkins.*

*"I thought he turned in," replied Strong, reaching for his tie at the foot of the bed.*

*"Something's bugging him, he can't sleep," said the head of the President's Secret Service detail. He shook his head. "Forget the haberdashery, he's in a* mood. *He wants you* now, *you know?"*

*The two men hustled down the corridor to the suite, where Strong, still stuffing his shirttail in, stood by while Simpkins tapped on the door.*

*"Mr. President? Strong is here. Do you still—"*

*"Definitely," said the President. "Send him in."*

*Strong found him dressed in a Japanese-style black-and-red kimono over clashing blue pajamas, pacing the two-inch carpet, holding a plastic glass of what appeared to be Ovaltine.*

"Good campaign day," said Strong, preemptively. "Big crowds, two governors' endorsements—"

"Should have been three," replied the President. "Forney had something in his eyes, I could see he didn't believe me about the Number-Two spot. Kept asking about Vandercleve. I told him to forget Vandercleve. He said, 'Hard to forget, he's all over the news.' Are you listening, Regis? All over the news! That Ivy League sonofabitch is up to something, no doubt about it."

The President took a swig of Ovaltine. Strong cleared his throat. "Forney's playing games," he said. "When the time comes—"

"And that phone call this morning," said the President, back turned to his chief of staff as he looked down on the night glow of a dozen Peachtree Streets. "That, Regis, was the last straw. Nobody's hung up on me in years. Not since"—he turned away from the picture window—"not since I asked Marlon Brando to head up my Artists and Entertainers Committee. And whose bright idea was that?"

"We were told at the time—"

"You were young then, Regis, new on the job," said the President, the cutting edge gone from his voice. "Sorry I mentioned it. We all make mistakes. But now"—the President took one last sip of his Ovaltine and gestured with the empty glass —"now we can't afford mistakes, can we? So after we get back to Washington—when?"

"Tomorrow night," replied Strong. "Six stops, in Florida, the Carolinas, Virginia. Then to Andrews, around eight P.M."

"Tomorrow night, fine. We go back, I get a good night's sleep in the Lincoln Room, wake up inspired, then I talk to Vandercleve. No ifs, ands, or hang-ups. Right?"

"Right," said Strong. He turned to leave.

"Marlon Brando," chuckled the President. "Can you imagine? I called all the way to Tahiti, at daytime rates. . . ."


*Transcript, Tape 109-Y, telephone conversation through Signal between Regis Strong, WH chief of staff, and Frank Lee, press secretary to the Vice President, 22 May (2315 hours).*

RS: Hello, Lee? Sorry we were interrupted, but we're in business. I've got the answer to all our problems.

FL: You do?

RS: Yeah, something the old man said about art and entertainment. That interruption—it was him, still chewing rugs about not talking to Vandercleve. So I just finished on the phone to Vegas—

FL: Vegas? Wait, before you get into that, we've got other problems.

RS: Such as?

FL: McCluskey's on the brink, his wife wants him to see a priest—

RS: McCluskey? Priest?

FL: And Percival, the headmaster at Barton Academy, he still wants the VP to deliver a speech, and the Second Lady wants to be surrogate, which would be a *(expletive deleted)* disaster—

RS: I said, slow down, you're hyperventilating. My call to Vegas takes care of the speech and call-in. You know Moishe Feinbaum?

FL: Feinbaum? The Vegas comic?

RS: The same. One of the President's strongest supporters, chairman of our Artists and Entertainers Committee. Second choice actually, but that's another story.

FL: The Man of a Thousand Voices?

RS: A Thousand and One. He's adding Bully Vandercleve to his repertoire and he's headed east on an Air Force 707 in one hour. Now do you read me?

FL: Feinbaum? On the phone?

RS:   Exactly. His plane lands at Andrews at seven-fifteen. He'll be picked up by Kurt Deutsch, head of our Special Operations Group, then taken to a safe-house in Northern Virginia. You'll be there, waiting.

FL:   I will?

RS:   Right. Deutsch picks you up at five-thirty, takes you there, then swings over to Andrews. That gives you, let's see, four hours sleep and enough time to shower, shave, dress, and get ready to rehearse our guest.

FL:   Rehearse him for what?

RS:   For starters, a phone call from the President.

FL:   I see. And—ah—how much does our guest know?

RS:   He knows his country needs him to carry out a supersecret mission.

FL:   National security?

RS:   What else? Feinbaum's one of those West Coast flakes who loves cloak-and-dagger *(expletive deleted)*. As a matter of fact, he loves everything. He loves this President, the last President, the next President. Humor him. Tell him he's indispensable.

FL:   So okay, he picks up the phone and talks to his pal, the President. And says what?

RS:   You tell, me, Lee. My job is to supply the equipment. Yours is to make it run. I don't give a *(expletive deleted)* what he says as long as Hertz is happy when he hangs up. But one thing for sure: you *(expletive deleted)* well better have a line on why your boss hasn't held a press conference to withdraw from the ticket.

FL:   I'll give it some thought.

RS:   You have six hours until our guest arrives. I'm turning in.

* * *

I'd seen Feinbaum's manic act on TV—who hasn't?—but in
person, only once. A memorable occasion:

## MOISHE (THE VOICE) TICKS OFF FIRST LADY

Headline, page 3 of the *Daily News,* the morning after the
Inaugural Gala. The Man of a Thousand Voices—call out any
name, any sex, he'll reproduce it, Memorex quality—had wowed
the crowd (and made the First Lady's Never Again list) with a
four-part impersonation of Prince Andrew, Fergie, Pee Wee Her-
man, and Bette Midler as a *ménage à quatre.*

But whether the President's wife liked him or not, Moishe
Feinbaum wasn't a talent to be ignored, least of all by Regis Strong,
who saw him as a link between the White House and that small
but influential show-biz coterie valued by politicians for fund-rais-
ing and other PR uses. When, for example, polls showed the
Leader of the Free World perceived by minority groups as a man
lacking warmth and compassion, it was Feinbaum to the rescue.
At the annual convention of the American Multi-Ethnic Society in
Wilkes-Barre, he humanized Hertz by eclectically greeting him
with an *abrazo,* a *salaam,* and a buss on both cheeks, topped—
with cameras rolling and the crowd bananas—by a high-and-low
five.

Feinbaum also enjoyed the unique privilege of calling the
President "Bubala," though that wasn't altogether surprising, since
he called everybody "Bubala." It was an affirmation of his eth-
nicity.

Oh, yes, a word about that: In the event you've spent the
last twenty years reading the *Christian Science Monitor* and
aren't looped into the Vegas scene, you may be under the impression that Moishe Feinbaum is an Ashkenazi Jew. Wrong. He is a
converted black ex-Baptist who (following the example set by Cas-
sius Clay/Muhammed Ali) made an appropriate name change
after turning in his platinum Bijan neck chain for a simple Star of
David.

# SOMEWHERE IN NORTHERN VIRGINIA

## MAY 23 (6:15 A.M.)

To get there, I sat, or rather lurched, cringing in the backseat of an altered-state limo—Rolls body with what I took to be a Stuka engine—over roads pitted with chassis busters, until my driver hung a right onto a twisting gravel path, went into sixth gear, then suddenly stopped, throwing me to the floor, where I lay cursing until he came around, lifted me out, removed my blindfold, and growled, "We're here, just don't ask where."

Kurt Deutsch, the head Handyman, was just as Sam Andreas had described him: a bull-chested atavist with a walrus mustache and a jagged scar across his right cheek, possibly a memento of service with the Green Berets, Da Nang, 1968, but more likely an *insigne d' honneur,* Hell's Angels, Monterey, 1970. He sported opaque sunglasses (K-mart), coordinated with a powder-gray suit (Sears), a fascisti-black designer shirt (Gabriel D'Annunzio), and a purple tie (Kresge's) featuring a Windsor knot the size of a mango. A man of few words, he preferred direct action, as when, on picking me up, he spun me around to apply the blindfold before I entered the limo. Only when I protested that we were on the same side did he speak, informing me that he knew that and had already made allowances. Unlike most random visitors to the safe-house, I'd only be sightless, not gagged, for the journey.

"Wait here," said Deutsch, as if I had an option; then he was off to Andrews Air Force Base in a cloud of gravel to pick up Feinbaum. I looked around. Not a bad-looking layout for an unauthorized clandestine White House operation. It was a sumptuous Virginia manor, stocked, I soon discovered, with the finest in victuals and furnished in French colonial, with an inscrutable cook-butler and (breaking the Gallic mold) a Nordic blonde of inordinate sensuality who, I surmised, was something more than safe-housekeeper whenever Deutsch had special guests. The cook was called Nu; the blonde, Helga.

It was a shortly after 6:00 A.M. when I arrived, and Nu graciously served me *café noir* with a delicate pinch of cinnamon—just what the doctor ordered to cut through the miasma brought on by a sleepless night. A complaint about a throbbing headache, an aftermath of Deutsch's madcap driving, brought forth two Tylenol, a bottle of Perrier, and the offer of a trapezius massage ministered by the safe-housekeeper. With a hard day ahead and given the importance of the job to the nation's security, I figured Mo would understand.

*"This is an unpardonable gaucherie."*
Somewhere out there, Winston Churchill was reproaching me.
*"See here, old chap, your illustrious guest has arrived and you seem to be comatose."*
Not Churchill anymore, but America's foremost conservative, and he was absolutely right. I had indeed dozed off, after only a few minutes of the dexterous Helga's hands-on therapy. Lifting an eyelid, I waved my masseuse away and said, "Let me guess—William F. Buckley."

"Actually, his son Chris," replied the wide-eyed gnome hovering over my chair. "What you might call"—he flung an invisible cape across his shoulder, in the manner of Bela Lugosi—"a *blawd* relation!" He uttered a manic whoop, bent at the waist to slap his blue velour pants knee, and in what I took to be his own voice, shrilled, "Love it, *love* it, LOVE it!" Then, clutching my hand and turning it palm up—as he had the President's that inspired night in Wilkes-Barre—he applied a damp-palmed low-five and said: "You Frank Lee, my tutor for a day?"

I nodded, yes. Kurt Deutsch, who'd been watching the scene with curled lip and bristling mustache, turned to leave. "You want anything," he muttered as he passed through the door, "I'll be inna next room."

"You want anything," repeated the Man of a Thousand Voices, uncannily mimicking the head Handyman, "I'll be inna next room." Again the crazed whoop and knee slap. "Love it, *love* it, LOVE it!" He jerked a ringed thumb toward the door. "Member of the Company?" he asked.

"Of a sort—" I began, only to be cut off by George Bush.

*"Love* that CIA," said Bush, transmogrifying into John Wayne in the next breath. "Now hear this, pilgrim. No sooner than the plane hits the tarmac, my driver there greets me with a *blindfold!*" Whoop, slap, and now the voice was Moishe Feinbaum's, none other. "We make tracks down the road, him doing Mario Andretti, me doing James Bond, both versions, Connery and Moore. Then a little JFK for variety. You know, 'Ask not what your country, da-dum, but what you, da-dum, da-dum,' and next thing out of the box, he *stops* the limo, *pulls* me out, and *gags* me for the rest of the trip!" Another whoop. "LOVE it! This is *my* kind o'town, Chicago is . . ."

He wheeled about the room, segueing from Sinatra to Willie Nelson; then, eyeing my masseuse, closed in to whisper, in the mode of early Jack Nicholson, "Stockholm's pride ain't too shabby. You got her signed to an exclusive?"

"Not at all, Mr. Feinbaum," I replied, eager to get a word in. "But that can wait. We have work to do."

*"Mr.* Feinbaum?" he replied, now Jimmy Swaggart on one knee. "Have mercy, brother! I was just idlin' my engine. She's all yours, my fellow American (FDR). I wouldn't *dream* of touching her (Gary Hart)." He rose, laid one hand across his spindly breastbone, raised the other, and intoned in the redoubtable voice of Richard Nixon, "May the Lord God Jehovah strike me dead if I lie."

He dropped to the floor, arms and legs splayed. "Last rites," he croaked, finally getting around to Cagney. "Is there a priest in the house? Pat O'Brien? Karl Malden? Faith, father, it's gettin' dark . . ."

"Moishe," I said, working a different approach. "You're the greatest, a living legend—several in fact—but what your country wants to know is—"

He was on his feet *instanter,* chest out, saluting.

"Can you do Vice President Vandercleve?"

He closed his eyes, drew a breath. "Bubala," he said; then, with chilling verisimilitude to my late master's voice, "would I be he-ah if I couldn't?"

Ten A.M.: While Feinbaum was in the next room fighting jet lag with a Nordic rubdown and I was working on a script for the

NBA locker-room call, Regis Strong phoned from Raleigh to remind me, as if I needed it, that in twenty-four hours Signal would be on the line with the President.

"The old man thinks he'll be talking to Vandercleve at his residence," said Strong. "How's Feinbaum doing?"

"Feinbaum's fine," I said. "As a matter of fact, he's having the time of his life."

"Oh yeah, Helga. I forgot."

"That and the line I fed him."

"You fed him a *what?*"

"Line, as in *story*. He thinks he's a key player in the biggest spy scam since the CIA planted a bug in Castro's beard. Your idea, remember? You said he's a spook buff, so I told him the KGB's put a tap on the President's phone, the Vice President's on a secret overseas mission—"

"Secret mission?"

"You know, like Kissinger in China, Ollie North in Tehran, Bush in Hanoi—"

"Bush in Hanoi? Never heard of it."

"Exactly. It was a *secret,* see? The same as Vice President Vandercleve's mission. We don't want the Russians to know about it, so with the KGB tapped in, the President is faking a call to the Vice President—"

"Jesus, you've almost got *me* believing it! Lee, for the first time, I hand it to you. . . . Wait a minute, other line's ringing. Got to hang up, the old man wants me."

### SONICS TAKE TITLE IN O/T, 102–98

—*Headline, Sports page,*
Washington Post

A script: I didn't have any problem working one up for the locker-room call because the formula for phone colloquies between the White House and winning coaches hasn't changed since Nixon perfected it in the late sixties.

*Transcript, Tape No. 123-D, telephone conversation through White House Signal between the Vice President and Bernie Bickerstaff, head coach, NBA champion Seattle SuperSonics, 23 May (2215 hours).*

VP:   Hello, Coach? Great game, great game. I just wanted you and your great team to know—

BB:   Mr. Vice President? Sorry, but I'm having a hard time hearing—

VP:   —what a great job you've done representing not only the great community of Seattle and the great state of Oregon but a great sport and the great American spirit of sacrifice and teamwork.

BB:   Sir, we've got a bad connection and I'm having—

VP:   So to you and yours, congratulations and godspeed! It was great! We loved it, *loved* it, LOVED it!


A little "improv" never hurt any performance, said Feinbaum. Debatable, but I had to concede that while the real Bully Vandercleve wouldn't be caught dead speaking Malibu English (he had no aptitude for foreign tongues), little Moishe's voice impression was convincing enough to make anything he said credible.

I know what you're thinking. Why Seattle, *Oregon?* Because if a Vice President didn't make *some* sort of gaffe in a public statement, it might look suspicious. So the locker-room call went off perfectly, complete with snide comments from two dozen disk jockeys around the country, an outraged blast from the mayor of Seattle, and a new Letterman joke.

That, however, was just a warm-up. Now came the big call, the one from the Oval Office. The challenge was, *What would the President say and when would he say it?* No telling, so I couldn't come up with a script. The next best thing, I figured, was a lexicon of political nonspeak—the routine buzzwords that pols use when they're conning their way past sticky issues.

I gave Feinbaum five all-purpose Washington phrases, *au courant* since the vacuous eighties: (1) "I hear you," (2) "I see where you're coming from," (3) "Good question," (4) "I'm still chewing on it," (5) "I'll get back to you."

With luck and a bad connection, they'd be enough to get even a West Coast flake through a ten-minute conversation in the Capital of the Free World.

*Transcript, Tape No. 204-X, telephone conversation through White House Signal between the President and the Vice President/24 May (1030 hours).*

SIGNAL:    Mr. Vice President? This is Signal. The President's on the line.

P:    Bully? Good to talk to you again. It's been some time.

VP:    I hear you.

P:    Yes. Well, I've been on the road campaigning, you know, and everywhere I go, this business about the Vice Presidential nomination comes up. I—uh—thought we'd reached an understanding.

VP:    I see where you're coming from.

P:    Well, didn't we?

VP:    Good question.

P:    You do recall our breakfast, don't you? You said you'd hold a news conference—

VP:    I'm still chewing on it.

P:    Still chewing on it? But more than two weeks have passed—

VP:    Excuse me a minute, a *(expletive deleted)* fly has been driving me ape—

P:    Hello?

VP: There, got the little *(expletive deleted)*. Now, you were saying—

P: I was saying, about the news conference, Vandercleve, and your *(expletive deleted)* withdrawal, that's what I was saying. I want your *(expletive deleted)* answer and I want it now! Understand?

VP: I hear you.

P: You hear me? What the *(expletive deleted)* is that supposed to mean?

VP: Mean? Well, like, I see where you're coming from, good question, I'm still chewing on it, I'll get back to you, the whole *(expletive deleted)* schmeer.

## THE OVAL OFFICE

MAY 24 (10:45 A.M.)

Chest heaving, the President cradled the phone, opened a side drawer, withdrew his pillbox, replaced it, opened another drawer, withdrew a flask, and handed it to his chief of staff.

"So, Regis," he said, as the chief of staff poured a jigger of Bombay gin into a shot glass, "you've been covering up, haven't you?" He bolted the shot, then made an ahhh sound as if kicked by a mule.

Strong, color draining, said nothing.

"Twenty-fifth amendment, isn't it?" said the President. Pause. "Well, isn't it? I'm fighting for my political life, on the verge of the biggest diplomatic meeting in a generation, everything up in the air, and now I need a new Vice President, right? Not next January, but today."

Slowly, hesitantly, Strong nodded.

The President rose from his chair and approached his chief of staff. "Now I understand why you wouldn't set up another meeting with Vandercleve," he said. "I appreciate it, Regis, you're trying to protect me, keep me from knowing the worst. But you should have known you couldn't fool your Commander-in-Chief—that sooner or later I'd find out."

Strong, avoiding eye contact, nodded mechanically.

"So what do we do now?" asked the President. "Tell me, what?" He walked to the bay window overlooking the south lawn and ran a quivering hand through his thin-thatched dyed-brown hair. "Middle of an election year, back to the wall, and I've got a frigging Vice President who's gone bonkers!"

*"While the Democrats will winnow their field to an even dozen, the Republican presidential race is too close to call."*

*—Pollster Duncan Trice on the upcoming Southern primaries, the "Today" show, May 25*

## THE VICE PRESIDENT'S PRESS OFFICE
MAY 25 (9:30 A.M.)

★ "The good news is that we're finally catching up on the Vice President's fan mail. The bad news is that he's just been named Father of the Month by the AmNukes. That means another five thousand letters to answer, not to mention the chauvinists still writing in because of his letter to Steinem—"

"Am-what?"

"AmNukes," repeated Carla. "The American Nuclear Family Association. A very influential group out West. They have their own cable show with an audience of millions, y' know?"

"Never heard of 'em," I said, doing a number with my Greek worry beads.

Carla turned a page to read another item from the White House morning news summary. "And Gregorio Marone—I guess you haven't heard of him either?"

"The man or the label?" I asked, still pondering the bad news coming out of the South. "Don't tell me—he's got the Vice President on his list of America's Ten Best-Dressed Men."

"The *World's* Ten Best-Dressed Men," replied Carla. "It's on all the wires. Twenty years in public life, Bully Vandercleve never drew an honorable mention for dress, much less parenting. Can you believe it?"

I tuned her out, absorbed by the headlines: "GRITS TUESDAY" DECISION DOUBTFUL, in the *Post,* and EXPERTS SEE NO CLEAR GOP WINNER, in the *Times.*

"He was only an ordinary dresser," Carla was saying. "No offense, Frank, but that was one part of the old image you didn't do much for. Oh, well. Sufficient unto the day—"

"Are the screw-ups thereof," I said, my eye fixed on another vexing headline: STANTON TO REOPEN WALL STREET HEARINGS.

"What's today's crisis? The Barton Academy speech?"

"That's tomorrow and besides, we've worked it out," I said. Subheadline: PANEL TO CALL C. FOSTER ABEL.

"Worked it out how? Don't tell me you're going with Feinbaum. After what he did on the call from Hertz? Want my advice?"

"No."

"Cancel the speech. Less than a week to go, what can Percival do?"

"Percival's not the problem. It's the Second Lady," I said, flipping to sports. METS ROUTED BY EXPOS, 11–0/DYKSTRA EJECTED. That settled it. There was nothing to do but go back home, roll out of the sack, and start the day over.

"The Second Lady?"

"She won't *let* me cancel," I said, stuffing the *Post,* all five sections, into the round file. "First, she wanted to make the speech herself, but Strong drew the line. God only knows what she'd say. So the compromise was, we tell Percival the Vice President is tied up on urgent matters in Washington—"

"National security?"

"National security—tied up in Washington and can't appear personally but will take time to deliver the commencement address via phone hookup. We sedate Feinbaum, put an Uzi to his head, decapitate his favorite Ferrari—whatever it takes to make him deliver the text as is."

"And the Second Lady?"

"She's on stage to pass out the goodies and get an honorary sheepskin herself. She'll be the first female in history with a Barton Academy diploma."

"And she'll settle for that? I doubt it."

I checked the *Times*'s sports section for a second opinion, discovered it also had the Mets losing 11–0 with Dykstra ejected, and stuffed it. Then: "Carla," I said, "you're a great deputy press secretary, and you may even have guessed right on 'Grits Tuesday,' but when it comes to Second Ladies, you don't know squat."

*Calls and more calls . . .*

There were 259 requests for interviews with the Vice President, up 25 since the start of trading at nine that morning. Only 2 deserved more than passing notice. The first was from Romana Clay, who told Carla she was "getting heat" from her network to get an exclusive with Vandercleve for the evening news. The second was from ever-reliable Ben Colfax. I stuffed both calls.

There were also five messages from sources outside the news media. Otto De Faye, Maximilian Mize, and C. Foster Abel had phoned at McCluskey's suggestion, which made three more to file and try to forget. But the last two couldn't be stuffed. Sam Andreas wanted to do a lunch. Sam could wait. Miriam Littlepaugh, calling from the Vice President's office, couldn't.

"Go over it again, Miriam, and *sloooowly*. What exactly did Lois McCluskey say?"

"That Mac was under the weather and wouldn't be in today."

McCluskey malingering? In all our years in Albany and Washington he'd never once missed a day's work. First in every A.M., last to leave every P.M. I hung up on Miriam, rather rudely I suppose, to call the McCluskey home. No answer, except:

*"Hello there. This is Lois McCluskey. Neither Martin nor I are chez nous at the moment but . . ."*

I hung up, again rather rudely, and punched Strong's number. Carla reentered, now flapping a memo that told of another call. *Your son,* it informed me, *is on line 3.*

Tommy's valedictory address!

Ms. Kaltenborn was on the line: "Mr. Strong's office."

How could I have forgotten?

"Hello? Mr. Strong's office."

What would I tell the kid? What *could* I tell the kid?

Ms. Kaltenborn hung up. I looked at Line 3, flashing. *Guilt-guilt-guilt.*

"Tell him," I said, eyes averted, "I'll get right back."

Carla snatched up the memo, shot me a disdainful, possibly even contemptuous look, and marched out, just as the string holding my worry beads snapped, spraying little blue pellets across the office floor.


*Transcript, Tape No. 154-B, telephone conversation between Regis Strong, WH chief of staff, and Frank Lee, press secretary to the Vice President, 25 May (1000 hours).*

FL:  We have a problem. Got a few minutes?

RS:  For you, all the time in the world. Just make it fast.

FL:  It's McCluskey. Remember, I told you his wife wanted him to see a priest?

RS:  So? Catholics see priests all the time. What about it? Hey, Lee! I've got a few primaries working tomorrow, and—

FL:   I know, but McCluskey didn't show up at the office this morning. I think he's—

RS:   Gone to see the priest. He's praying. So?

FL:   Confessing.

RS:   Say again?

FL:   Confession. Hello?

RS:   I'm letting it sink in. What you're saying is that McCluskey's adding somebody outside the loop to the Need-to-Know list. Hmmmmm . . . Where does he live, what church does he attend? Never mind, I can computer check it.

FL:   His wife called Miriam Littlepaugh just a few minutes ago. I couldn't reach them at home. They must have just left—

RS:   Got it, right here. Saint Ignatius, northwest D.C. That's about, I'd say, twelve minutes away. . . . Deutsch can do it in nine, beat them to the church, easy.

FL:   Deutsch? What's he got to do with it? Hello, Strong? Hello?

## EN ROUTE TO FLORA'S JOINT, ARBUTUS, MARYLAND

MAY 25 (1:30 p.m.)

Kim's Deli was now off-limits, Sam informed me. Bugged since we'd last been there. Strong, he said, had gone paranoid. There wasn't a restaurant, pizzeria, doughnut shop, or fast-food establishment within twenty miles of the White House that hadn't been wired for sound. What about a simple hot dog in the park? Not safe, said Sam. One of every four street people in Washington was on the take from Deutsch's Handymen. Even the city's pigeon population, strutting about Lafayette Square, Dupont Circle, and Cleveland Park, couldn't be trusted.

"Wired," explained Sam, as we sped up the Baltimore-Washington Parkway to a new haunt. "One of our agents snatched up a pigeon from the ledge outside our office last week. Sonofabitch was wired to the gills."

"Gills?"

"Tailfeathers, whatever. Don't know who did it. Russians, Libyans, Cubans, but gut instinct tells me it was the Handymen. Can't be too careful dealing with those bastards."

"So I've noticed," I said, as we veered into the exit leading to Greenbelt. "Where are we going? Didn't you tell me Flora's Joint was straight up the road?"

"It is."

"Then why did we take the Greenbelt exit?"

"There's been a car back of us ever since we left the Washington city limits," explained Sam. "Could be a tail."

"Or just somebody driving to Baltimore."

Sam shook his head. "Orioles don't play till tonight," he replied.

"Maybe he's going to Baltimore for some other reason."

"Name one," said Sam, as he glanced at the rearview mirror.

"Little Italy."

"Possible," he said, eyes still on the mirror. "Good restaurants. But the car didn't look the type."

Having now detoured three miles, we reversed course to reenter the parkway, Sam nodding in self-approval at having lost our pursuer. "Like I always tell you, Lee, you can't take anything for granted these days."

At long last we were coming around to the reason for his call.

"We've been getting a lot of threatening letters in the Vice President's file the last couple of weeks," he said. "More threats than he got when he was alive. You know why?"

"Nuts," I replied, suddenly remembering I hadn't eaten anything since 6:30 that morning. Sam now veered off at the Beltsville exit, to lose a trailing family Winnebago he viewed as suspicious, if indeed not life-threatening.

"Right, nuts," he said. "They've noticed all the media play the Vice President's been getting lately, so he's become controversial. What we call HPP—a High Profile Protectee. You know what that means?"

"I'll bite," I said, a Freudian slip as I contemplated what manner of fare would be dispensed at Flora's Joint. Italian? Greek? Kosher? (Not, I was certain, Korean.)

"It means, going by the books, we've got to assign more men to the detail."

"How many more?" I asked, as we again backtracked.

"Ten, maybe a dozen."

Ten, maybe a dozen more for the Need-to-Know list. My intimate little conspiracy had grown, first to battalion, now to regiment size.

"No problem with keeping their traps shut," said Sam, reading my thoughts. "The old hands know it's a dummy detail to protect the Vice President's name and the new agents don't ask questions. They figure it's some kind of training exercise. But the problem is . . ."

Finally. We were getting to the point as well as our lunch stop. A highway marker, ARBUTUS EXIT ½ MILE, flashed by.

"The problem is, I have to make up next month's manpower roster. Even when the Demos trim their field to a dozen, that's still a lot of protectees to cover. We're spread thin. So my question is . . ."

ARBUTUS NEXT EXIT

". . . what are your plans after Grits Tuesday?"

"Plans?"

"The Southern vote won't settle a damn thing. Strong's gonna ask you to keep the operation going, probably to the convention. So—"

We shot past the Arbutus exit.

"Sam," I pointed out, "you just missed our turnoff."

"We're not going to Flora's Joint," he grimaced. "I just said that to throw the Handymen off when we left the EOB."

I'd forgotten. Not only was the EOB *surveilled,* but there were pigeons nearby as we entered the car.

"Then where *are* we going, and how long will it take?"

"You'll see when we get there," said Sam. "Just tell me so I can make out my summer roster. What are your plans for June?"

"First, yours," I replied wondering whether the Service would go along with what amounted to a four-week extension of Operation Avis.

We swung off the parkway again.

"I don't think you've been listening, Lee. I said threats against the protectee are higher than we've ever had for any Vice President. The nuts are out in force. You should see the letters. Gonna shoot, blow up, hang, defenestrate—"

"Interesting," I said, distracted by my growling innards. "I never realized Gloria Steinem had violence-prone friends."

"It hasn't got anything to do with Steinem or that columnist," replied Sam. We circled back to the parkway, headed for Baltimore. "It's the nut mentality. They're looking for a challenge, see? Something to get them on the evening news. Nobody's ever shot a Vice President before. Presidents, popes, senators, governors, preachers, rock musicians, *they've* been shot. But *never* a Vice President. It would be a Guinness first. Which means, if you decide to go along with Strong after Grits Tuesday—not that I'm encouraging it—that like it or not, we go along."

"That's good of you, Sam," I said. "Frankly, I had my doubts—"

"It's the code, you know?" said Sam, as we entered the Baltimore city limits. "The Service can't walk away from an HPP. Dead or not, the man is our protectee."

We turned right and entered Little Italy, where he dropped me off in front of Sabatino's.

"See you in a few minutes," he said. "Got to circle round, make sure we haven't been tailed."

## THE VICE PRESIDENT'S OFFICE
MAY 25 (6:45 P.M.)

Zuppa del mare, linguini with clam sauce, veal Milanese, rugala al Sinatra, half a carafe of Ruffino Ducale, and a touch of capuccino amoretto to top it off. Grazie. I deserved it. The day had been rough, and it was only half over.

First, there was the long journey home: Baltimore to Washington by way of the Civil War battlefields of southern Pennsylvania and western Maryland. Sam was certain he'd spotted a half dozen tailing vehicles, and it made no difference that we were simply headed back to the White House–EOB. It was the principle of the thing. Whenever they (whoever "they" might be) put a tail on you, you lost it. Let him (whoever "he" might be) go back to his boss and explain that Sam Andreas had given him the slip—*again*.

We reached the D.C. city limits at 5:15. From there to the White House–EOB was normally a twenty-minute drive, thirty-five in rush hour; but Sam, still wary, thought it might be a good idea to park the car three miles from the office and finish the trip via separate cabs. Once in my cab I gave the driver my destination, sat back, and promptly fell asleep; only to wake up thirty minutes later, circling RFK Stadium. My cabbie, it seemed, was new to the city, spoke only a dozen words of English (Hello. Good-bye. Where to? Thank you. You're welcome. I don't make change), and didn't have the slightest idea where (or what) the White House was.

I debarked, recorded the name and number of his vehicle (All-American Cabs/No. 176), gave him a fiver for his trouble to avoid a nasty bilingual argument, and tramped to the Metro. Once back at the office—my staff had long gone—I found two red-tagged items Scotch-taped to my phone; the only sure way, Carla knew, that I'd ever see them:

**1.** McCluskey had phoned at 2:25 to say he was feeling better and would be in tomorrow. Vast relief. Sam had been right. He'd said that, contrary to my worst fears, Deutsch wouldn't hurt Mac ("*Kidnap* maybe," he reassured me, "but not *terminate.*")

**2.**     An Eyes Only memo from Carla that had me reaching for the phone before I got to the bottom line. . . .

**MEMORANDUM**

# OFFICE OF THE VICE PRESIDENT
## WASHINGTON

CODE RED: *BURN-WHILE-READING*

**TO:**        FL
**FROM:**     CB
**SUBJECT:**  OTTO DE FAYE DROP-BY

May 25

The above-named subject, unarmed but dangerous, appeared at the press office door at 1530 today, while you were on your extended lunch break. Demanded to see you, but was persuaded to deal with me on an "utmost confidential basis" re his (direct quote) "longtime client and dear friend, Vice President Vandercleve."

His "dear friend," says De Faye, "has not availed himself of my *sty-a-ling* services in over a fortnight" (emphasis supplied). Was I aware of the fact that the VP thinks so highly of those services, not to mention those of his house manicurist, Angelica LeBlanc, that they are included as part of his official traveling party in overseas trips? (Usually, as I recall, when the Second Lady didn't go. Remember Angelica? *Washingtonian* magazine swimsuit cover, two years running.)

So far, no problem. Maybe, I suggested, the VP has been too busy to get styled-and-filed in recent weeks. Not so, said De Faye, letting the big shoe drop: Yesterday afternoon, he said, after giving the President his weekly shear-and-dye job up in the Oval Office, he hung around the White House–EOB complex, waiting to take the issue up with the VP when he left for the day. But (direct quote), "While I saw the Vice President's retinue leave, I didn't see *him!*" See your optometrist, I said. You missed him in the swirl. Direct quote: "There is *nothing* wrong with my vision, Ms. Whatever-your-name-is! You can't fool a man's hairstylist! If I know anything at all, I know my clients' heads, and I assure you, *the Vice President's coif was not in that motley crowd!*" (Emphasis supplied.)

At this point in time, your son called in again, taking me off the hook. The way I left it with De Faye, you're to get back to him with a reasonable explanation ASAP.

Much luck.


*Transcript, Tape No. 126-C, telephone conversation through Signal switchboard between Regis Strong, WH chief of staff, and Frank Lee, press secretary to the Vice President, 25 May (1855 hours).*

SIGNAL:  Mr. Strong? This is Signal. Mr. Lee's on the line.

RS:  Lee? Glad you called. I was about to get in touch. We've got to get together first thing in the morning. A problem's come up—

FL:  You're telling me? De Faye—

RS:  What?

FL:  Otto De Faye. Who'd have thought the whole thing could blow because of a *(expletive deleted)* barber?

RS:     Lee, this is beginning to remind me of other conversations we've had. Just when I start thinking you've got your *(expletive deleted)* together, you come on like a rumhead. Speaking of which, what were you doing at Sabatino's this afternoon? Killing, as I understand it, half a bottle of red.

FL:     *(Inaudible)*

RS:     Listen, friend, one thing this operation doesn't need is another McCluskey. No crack-ups until the nomination is bagged, understand? Now what's this *(expletive deleted)* about De Faye the barber?

FL:     Just that—uh—he could be big-time trouble.

RS:     De Faye, trouble? Yeah, sure. Listen, you've had a couple hard days. Get a good night's sleep and see me, say, seven in the morning. Okay?

FL:     Okay, sure. Just answer—uh—one question. How did you know about the, uh . . .?

RS:     Sabatino's? My wife's family's from Baltimore. She was up there visiting. You know what they say, chum. In this business you can't be too careful. Be here at seven.


*"Arise, Young America!"*

Grabby speech title. Not necessarily one I'd have picked for a valedictory, but it was Tommy's call, and who was I (ranked 112th in a high school of class of 220) to quibble titles with a boy genius?

*My remarks today will be brief, directed not so much at the challenges facing the small word of academia as those confronting the larger universe outside—the real world that awaits all young Americans who leave high school and college in this watershed year of history.*

Hmmmm . . .

*I don't intend to mince words or principles. For what I say must be said—not tomorrow, but today—in a society that finds the ever-widening gap between rich and poor, the privileged and the needy . . .*

On second thought, too grabby. With time to spare I might have counseled a lighter touch. But who had time? It was a little after seven, the tail end of a dog day. I was beat, fighting to keep my lids up. Mo and Tommy were at home. I'd called in, groveled my apologies, and promised to arrive no later than eight with Father's definitive word on what had escalated into a major family issue: *The Speech!*

There were only five pages, double-spaced. It wouldn't take more than ten minutes to zip through, even if I was rusty at editing other people's speeches. We hadn't used a full-time wordsmith in the Vice President's office since Bully, weary of Nat Mabry's penchant for overworked Churchill quotes, had dumped him, with high recommendation, on an unsuspecting freshman senator.

*This, as we know, is commencement season. Throughout America hundreds of speeches will be delivered in the weeks ahead by pompous political and academic windbags, braying bromidic bullshit . . .*

That style! Unmistakable. The boy had been sneak reading Spiro Agnew, circa 1970.

*They talk drivel, while values shrivel. They obfuscate, while problems percolate. They dither, while young dreams wither.*

Also Jesse Jackson in full cry, circa 1984–88.

I reached instinctively, if groggily, for a blue pencil, then reconsidered. No, that would be parental censorship, hardly the way to persuade a headstrong youngster of the error of his eloquence. The thing to do was sneak up on the boy's pseudointellectual side. Gently point out that alliteration, like random rhyming, was forensically passé.

I put down the blue pencil and turned the page. A blur— *Proudhon . . . property . . . shackles . . .* Overheated rhetoric, had to be brought down to room temperature. . . . But first, forty winks. . . . Ten minutes on the office couch, that's all I'd need.

Then, up with a clear head, finish the speech, a twenty-minute drive . . . I'd be home by eight with time to spare.

*Arise, Young America!* By all means. But first forty, maybe forty-five, winks for a tired flack. . . .

*Transcript, Tape No. 164-Y, telephone conversation through Signal switchboard between Frank Lee, press secretary to the Vice President, and Maureen Lee, 26 May (0715 hours).*

SIGNAL:  Mr. Lee? Your wife has been trying to find you. She's on the line.

ML:  Frank, they've been looking all over. Regis Strong's secretary called to say you were late—

FL:  Wha—? Late? What time is it?

ML:  Seven-fifteen.

FL:  Seven-fifteen? No, not late at all. I've got forty-five minutes to get home. You and Tommy still—

ML:  Frank, seven-fifteen A.M. We waited up but—

FL:  Morning?

ML:  Morning. You were supposed to be at Strong's office at seven. Sleeping at the office? Frank, you've been pushing yourself too hard lately. I don't know what's wrong but something tells me—

FL:  Seven-fifteen? I was supposed to be at Strong's at seven. Jesus—

SIGNAL:  Mr. Lee? Pardon me, sir, for interrupting, but I just notified Mr. Strong's office we located you and—

FL:  Tell him, tell him I'll be right over. Mo? Sorry about last night, but—Mo? Mo?

# THE WHITE HOUSE WEST WING

## MAY 26 (7:30 A.M.)

I'd been there before looking like hell after a hard day and tough night. But the difference this time was that once inside the office I was warmed not only by Mrs. Kaltenborn's coffee but hot confections direct from Watergate Bakery, a gustatory treat usually reserved for Very Important Visitors.

"Sorry I'm late," I said, lifting a palmière from the silver tray.

"Don't mention it," said Strong, waving Mrs. K. out of the room. "The President's on the road, playing out the string down South, so I've got a little time to spare. Somebody has to take care of the store, you know? Clean up the mess, take inventory for a busy June. See the morning *Post?*"

He held up the front page.

### GOP DILEMMA: BITTER FIGHT
### LEADING UP TO CONVENTION

"So," he said, putting down the paper and picking up his desk calendar, "the question is, can you hack it? Have another sweet roll."

"Hack what?" I replied, playing dumber than he thought I was, though I didn't resent that as much as his low estimate of my selling price. Another sweet roll indeed!

Strong studied the calendar. "Convention's a two-day affair this year, streamlined for the tube," he said. "Monday keynote, platform, and nominations. Tuesday, the fourth, wrap it up with the vote for President and Vice President. Fireworks that night, a real TV extravaganza. Provided—are you *sure* you don't want another sweet roll?"

"Palmière," I corrected, deciding to hell with it. Since I'd

★ 119 ★

known for days what my answer would be, it wasn't really a sellout. "And while we're at it," I added, "another cup of coffee."

Strong pressed a button, which brought Mrs. K. back with a steaming refill. "Just leave the pot and hold my calls," he told her. "Mr. Lee and I have a lot to talk about this morning."

"The President is due to phone in from Plains in fifteen minutes," she replied. "Do you want—"

"Plains? What the hell's he doing—Oh, yeah. Touring the Carter Museum with Jimmy. No, tell him I got called to Capitol Hill or something. He'll be in a foul mood, not fit to talk to after the tour." Strong looked toward me. "He hates those bipartisan gestures, you know? But we need the crossovers."

"Should I say something came up on the anti-Castro resolution?" she asked.

"Perfect," said Strong. "Just don't make too much of it. Let's not get the man overwrought."

A credible lie to the President having been shaped, Mrs. Kaltenborn left and Strong's attention returned to his desk calendar. "The way I see it, you make your announcement about your boss on, say, Saturday, July first. We should definitely have it wrapped up by then. Hmmmm . . . five days left in May, thirty in June, one in July. That makes how many in all?

"Running mates or days?" I asked, biting into my second tasty bribe of the morning.

Strong studied the calendar, then squinted at the crystal chandelier overhead. "Thirty-five, thirty-six days, depending on the news cycle. July first is perfect. Enough lead time so that it won't put a damper on the convention festivities." He rubbed his chin. "Though come to think of it, a moment of silence would make great video. Say, just before the keynote. What are your thoughts on that, Lee?"

"On the moment of silence or the thirty-five days?" I asked.

"The moment, of course," Strong replied. "Your professional judgment. The thirty-five days? Hey, Lee, that should be a snap. Look what you've done in only two weeks! Given a month, who knows? You might even get your boss a *Time* cover."

Odd he should mention that. *Time* was the one cover Bully never made while alive. It was an omission he never failed to mention when in a mood to list my shortcomings as an alter ego. Responding, I'd point to my success in getting him cover stories in *Newsweek* and *US News & World Report.* But never *Time,* and the snub rankled him. Almost (though not quite) as much as being passed over three times for the presidency.


*Transcript, sworn testimony of C. Foster Abel before a closed session of the Senate Committee on Investment Fraud/26 May (0900 hours).*

SENATOR STARK: The Committee will come to order. Let the record show that we are proceeding in the absence of the Chairman, the gentleman from Ohio. It is my understanding, however, that Senator Stanton will be present when public televised hearings commence next Wednesday. Will the witness please identify himself?

MR. ABEL: I am C. Foster Abel, senior partner in the law firm of Delavan, Waterman, and Abel of New York City. I am accompanied here today by counsel, Mr. Lucius Cartwright of Washington, D.C.

SENATOR STARK: Has the witness been sworn?

CLERK: Yes, sir.

SENATOR STARK: Mr. Abel, you understand, don't you, that the purpose of this closed hearing is to prepare both you and the Committee for next week's open hearing—

MR. CARTWRIGHT: Senator, with all due respect, let's get on with it. My client has an eleven o'clock shuttle to catch.

SENATOR STARK: Very well then. I presume the witness has brought with him the documents requested by

|  |  |
|---|---|
| | the Committee, relating to stock transactions made during the past twenty-four months on behalf of Vice President Vandercleve? |
| MR. ABEL: | Senator, if I may— |
| MR. CARTWRIGHT: | Wait a minute, you don't have to answer that. Senator, with all due respect, the Committee has in its possession a sworn statement indicating that my client is the chief investor and sole executor of the Vice President's blind trust. Right or wrong? |
| SENATOR STARK: | I believe— |
| MR. CARTWRIGHT: | What, "believe"? You know. I turned the statement over to you just ten minutes ago. We take the position—and we might as well get this straight at the outset—that any inquiry into my client's transactions within the scope of that trust is beyond the jurisdiction of this Committee. |
| SENATOR STARK: | Oh, and may I ask under what specific statute that claim is made? |
| MR. ABEL: | I really think— |
| MR. CARTWRIGHT: | We don't need a specific statute. Our claim is made under the well-recognized common law right of executor's privilege. |
| SENATOR STARK: | Mr. Abel? Is that your claim? |
| MR. CARTWRIGHT: | With all due respect, Senator, I'd appreciate your directing that question to me. |
| SENATOR STARK: | The Committee is interested in hearing from the witness himself. |
| MR. CARTWRIGHT: | So what am I, a potted petunia? |

| | |
|---|---|
| MR. ABEL: | Lucius, really, I don't mind— |
| MR. CARTWRIGHT: | No, let's get this straight, before this farce goes public. I won't sit here and see this Committee run roughshod over my client's rights under the First, Fifth, Seventh, and Tenth Amendments to the Constitution. Are you familiar with those amendments, Senator, or do I have to spell them out? |
| SENATOR STARK: | If the witness and his counsel will excuse me, I'd like to discuss this turn of events with other members of the Committee. |
| MR. CARTWRIGHT: | Go right ahead. Just so we're out in time for Mr. Abel to catch his plane. |
| MR. ABEL: | Lucius— |
| SENATOR STARK: | Mr. Abel, Mr. Cartwright, I've been directed by the Committee, in the absence of our permanent Chairman, Senator Stanton, to order you to produce, forthwith, all documents relating to stock transactions made by the witness on behalf of Vice President Vandercleve over the past twenty-four months. |
| MR. ABEL: | Senator— |
| MR. CARTWRIGHT: | Wait, I'll handle this. Senator, with all due respect, this Committee has no legal or moral right to get its publicity-seeking hands on those papers. |
| MR. ABEL: | Lucius, please— |
| MR. CARTWRIGHT: | Furthermore, be forewarned that the Committee won't get those papers without a court fight. A long, expensive court fight, but one my client is prepared to make on behalf of the principle involved. |

| | |
|---|---|
| SENATOR STARK: | Mr. Abel? Is that your position? |
| MR. ABEL: | *(After conferring with counsel)* Yes, well, on advice of counsel, I respectfully decline— |
| SENATOR STARK: | Well, be assured, we mean to get to the bottom of this matter, to learn the truth— |
| MR. CARTWRIGHT: | A vendetta, a publicity circus. |
| SENATOR STARK: | As I was saying, to learn the truth, and given the witness's refusal to cooperate, we have no alternative but to summon the only other person familiar with the transactions at issue— |
| MR. ABEL: | Senator, if I may— |
| MR. CARTWRIGHT: | Relax, they're bluffing. |
| SENATOR STARK: | Oh? As I was saying, to summon the only other person familiar with the transactions at issue— |
| MR. CARTWRIGHT: | What a farce. |
| SENATOR STARK: | Vice President Vandercleve himself. |

## THE WHITE HOUSE WEST WING

MAY 26 (9:15 A.M.)

"Sorry for the interruption," said Strong, breezing back into the room. He ran a manicured hand across his brow, then checked his Rolex. "Whew! Should've followed my first instinct and not talked to the old man. You know what he's had me doing the past hour? Talking to senators, arm-twisting, stroking." He slid into his chair. "Goddamned anti-Castro resolution's got him climbing walls. Right-wing wackos could screw up the summit."

The intercom buzzed. Strong pressed a button.

"A call from Air Force One," said the disembodied voice of Mrs. Kaltenborn. "The President wants—"

"Tell him I'm on the phone with Senator Newmark," said Strong. "Closing the sale, getting Newmark off the fence. He'll buy that."

He pressed the button again, sat back, and ground his teeth. "Newmark," he muttered. "That cracker Cato could make the difference in a close vote." Then, looking at me for the first time since he'd entered the room: "Now where were we? Problems. You were saying, we've got problems. McCluskey and De Faye, is that all?"

*"All?"* I said. "Well, for starters, McCluskey is—"

"No problem," said Strong, opening a desk drawer and pulling out a button-sized cylinder. "It's under control, right here on tape. You want a listen?"

"To what?"

"What McCluskey told his priest," replied Strong. He gave the tape a fond, almost avuncular look. "Deutsch beat him to the church by a good ten minutes. Came on as a fire inspector, then slipped away, planted the mike—"

"You bugged a Confessional?" I asked, making abject silent apology to my paranoid friend Sam Andreas. "Just like that?"

*"Surveilled,"* Strong said irritably. "And it wasn't 'just like that.' Deutsch is a *talent,* one of the best in his field. Graduated Advanced Surveillance School magna cum liddy. But back to the tape. Very interesting. I'd heard one-on-ones between psychiatrists and patients, but never between a priest and a penitent. It's a totally new learning experience. Care to hear it?"

"No, thanks," I replied. "Just the bottom line."

"Well, you really had to be there, but you want bottom line, you get bottom line: McCluskey comes in sobbing, tells his story— Vice President Vandercleve is dead, there's a conspiracy to cover it up, the White House is in on it, the Second Lady is in on it—"

The intercom buzzed.

"The President again," said Mrs. Kaltenborn. "He wants to know how it went with Senator Newmark."

"Tell him Newmark's leaning our way," said Strong. "He's beginning to see how Castro's addressing a joint session might be good for the Alabama poultry industry. And Mrs. K.—"

"Yes?"

"If the old man calls back, tell him I'm on the Hill."

Strong rolled his eyes toward the ceiling. "Okay," he said, "picking it up. . . . So McCluskey goes on with his story, with the priest, a Father Teeley, saying 'Yes' and 'You don't say'—really, Lee, you should hear the tape to catch the good father's tone. You sure you don't—

"Positive," I said.

Strong shrugged. *"Chacun à son gout,"* he said. "So McCluskey finishes his spiel, and the priest is quiet a full minute, maybe two. Then he quotes Scripture: 'And the wild asses did stand in the high places'; which, frankly, escapes me, but then, I'm not religious, you know? Then the priest says, 'Strange are the ways of the secular world.' Meaning, God knows what."

"Then?"

"He asks McCluskey if he has anything else to confess, and McCluskey says, one, he's used the Lord's name in vain, and two, he's taken to drink for the first time in his life. At which point the priest says, 'I *seeeee,'* as if a great light's dawned."

The intercom again. Mrs. Kaltenborn: "The President wants to know where he can reach you on Capitol Hill," she said. "What should I tell him?"

"That I've dropped by the Vice President's office in the Capitol," replied Strong. "I doubt he'll call me there."

"McCluskey," I said, noting he'd lost his train of thought.

"Oh, yeah, bottom line. One Our Father and one Hail Mary on each blasphemy count, sprung on the drinking charge, provided he joins a church support group and doesn't go around repeating that story about the Vice President. 'Some people,' said the good Father Teeley, 'might not understand.' "

# BARTON ACADEMY
## MAY 26 (9:30 A.M.)

*Royce Percival was nervous. More nervous than usual, which said something about the importance of the occasion. Barton's headmaster, even on a normal schoolday, was a man who carried a portable panic button in his Brooks Brothers vest pocket.*

*What was important about today's commencement wasn't simply that Barton was turning another class of future leaders loose on society, but that among the members of this year's class was "Little Bubba" Tyrrell, only son of "Big Bubba" Tyrrell, the wealthiest real estate developer in the Southwest. He would be the first "Bubba," big or little, ever graduated by the Academy in its 150 years of existence; the first to ascend not to an Ivy League or proper Eastern school but an outlanders' college, West Tulsa State.*

*Hard to believe that a Barton product would seek higher education beyond the Hudson–Charles River perimeter, but times and standards had changed. Barton could no longer rely on old money for its operating funds, so the admission barriers were down, allowing the bright (and sometimes, as in Little Bubba's case, not-too-bright) scions of back country nouveaux to mingle with the Mayflower gentry.*

*For all his billions, Big Bubba was the paradigmatic parvenu that Percival had been brought up to disdain. But better the nouveau riche, as the headmaster once said (actually lifted) than no riche at all, and Barton, for all its reputation, desperately needed endowment money.*

*Big Bubba would be in the audience today, bursting with paternal pride over the sight and sound of a Tyrrell, only one generation removed from Oklahoma crude, getting a Barton diploma. And after the ceremonies, the land developer called "The Donald Trump of the Sun Belt" would meet privately with the* headmaster to discuss the Academy's financial needs, not only for this year but many years to come.

That was why Percival had held out for his old friend Bully Vandercleve as this year's commencement speaker, though some members of the Barton board wanted to bring in a substitute. A Nobel Prize winner was available to speak on short notice, they pointed out, as well as one of America's most distinguished statesmen-emeriti, ex-Secretary of State Ambrose Leffingwell. But Percival knew that an Establishment Vice President of the United States, even speaking by amplified sound in absentia, would impress Big Bubba more than any number of effete intellectuals or striped-pants cookie pushers. Especially when the Second Lady of the land would be onstage to hand Little Bubba his diploma.

"So glad you could be with us today," the headmaster fawned, extending a damp hand to Cissy Vandercleve as she arrived at Armistead Green, the traditional site of Barton's outdoor ceremonials. He led the Second Lady toward the stage. "I trust you left my dear friend Bully in good spirits," said Percival. "We do appreciate his finding time to speak to our graduates today."

"My husband was in excellent spirits when I last saw him," replied the Second Lady, looking beyond the headmaster's shoulder to count the house. About 300, she estimated, not including the graduates, who were filing in. "I'm sure he'd like to be here today, but—" She smiled her tight-lipped smile.

"Yesss," purred the headmaster, locating the Second Lady's front-row chair. "And did he, perchance, send a copy of his text along? This being Friday, our town editor—you're familiar, I know, with the Barton Weekly Eagle—is on deadline. He was hoping—"

"For a special occasion like this, the Vice President prefers to speak extemporaneously, from the heart," Cissy Vandercleve replied. "But if your editor is interested, I do happen to have an extra copy of my own remarks."

"Oh?" said Percival, watching the Second Lady rummage

*through her Louis Vuitton. "I didn't know you intended to favor us with any—uh—remarks."*

*"A brief message," Cissy Vandercleve replied, now dazzling the headmaster with her most toothsome smile. "My husband and I often speak in tandem on special occasions."*

## THE WHITE HOUSE WEST WING

### MAY 26 (10 A.M.)

*"De Faye!"* Strong barked the name. "I'd have *cut* that damned busybody's access years ago, but the President thinks he's the best hair dye–and–shampoo man east of L.A. Say again, he saw what?"

"Nothing," I replied. "That's the point. He went looking for the Vice President and couldn't find him in the crowd. Just the Secret Service detail—"

Strong held up a hand, as if struck by inspiration. He walked to the window, looked down at the Vice President's parked limo on West Executive Avenue, and muttered something about pissants mucking up process. Then he returned to his desk and pressed the button summoning Mrs. Kaltenborn.

"Dictation," he said, "for the President's signature."

"The President's private stock or official White House letter-head?" she asked.

"Official," replied Strong. He turned to me, as if I were privy to his devious inner thoughts. "De Faye could talk all right," he said. "That's what he does best, *talk.* Biggest blab in Washington. Cuts-and-talks, cuts-and-talks. That's why I stopped using him. He talks so much he forgets he's *cutting.*"

Mrs. Kaltenborn returned to the room, dictation pad and pen set to go.

"The only thing that'll keep De Faye from talking is a personal note from the President," said Strong. "Confidential, on official stationery. If we send the note on the *President's* letterhead, he'd show it around. Can't help himself. But make it official, ah!"— Strong held a finger to his head—"Then he thinks he's more than a friend, he's a member of the President's White House *team.* Practically a Cabinet member. You ready, Mrs. K? For openers, *Dear Otto . . ."*

# THE WHITE HOUSE

## WASHINGTON

May 26

*PERSONAL AND CONFIDENTIAL*

The Honorable Otto De Faye
c/o The De Faye Way Salon
1928 Northington Drive
City

Dear Otto:

A personal request, not simply as your friend and longtime client, but your President and Commander-in-Chief:

Specifically, it has come to my attention that your ever-keen eye has discerned the absence of your client and our mutual friend, the Vice President, from the Vice Presidential retinue leaving the Executive Office Building several days ago. I can well understand your perplexity, but write to assure you that there is indeed an explanation—one which will, in due time, become perfectly clear.

Suffice it to say, for the present, that you are in possession of information which, if made prematurely public, could do inestimable harm to the security of our nation and indeed the future of Western civilization as we know it.

You were right, incidentally, about the First Lady's shampoo. The new formula you recommended has done wonders for her morale.

With warm regards, I remain,

Yours in utmost confidence,

*[signature]*

## BARTON ACADEMY
### MAY 26 (10:20 A.M.)

*Power to the people? Land reform in the Third World?*

*Frantically, Royce Percival sought eye contact with someone, anyone who might pull the plug on the sound system. But the only eye he seemed to catch was that of Big Bubba Tyrrell, glaring at him from the first row of the Distinguished Visitors section.*

*Members of this year's graduating class, the speaker was saying, must "recapture the revolutionary spirit that infused young Americans in the decade of the sixties"; they must "throw off the shackles of mindless Yuppie conformity"; dedicate themselves, from this day forward, "to radical reform of the country's institutions," and not just by talk but by action because (Barton's headmaster rose halfway in his chair, ready to leave the stage and pull the plug himself), "action talks and bullshit walks."*

*The Vice President of the United States? Unbelievable. But there was no mistaking that voice, that cadence, that nasal inflection. Percival had always heard that sustained exposure to the American Vice Presidency could transmogrify those who held the office. But this, from Bully Vandercleve?*

★ **131** ★

*Cheers. Shouts from the graduating class of "Way to go, Bully!" A standing ovation. Not so much at what this year's commencement speaker had said, Percival surmised, as the fact that unlike 149 previous Barton Academy commencement speakers, he had said anything at all.*

*Mercifully, it was over. Percival only half-heard the peroration, some obscure 19th century definition of property, for he was already on his feet, moving toward the rostrum, anxious to get it over with. Hand out the diplomas, get an earful of Big Bubba Tyrrell's barnyard blasphemies, take his medicine from the board he'd overruled by insisting that his good friend Bully be this year's commencement speaker.*

*He turned toward the Second Lady, there to pass out the diplomas. She had a tight, inscrutable smile on her face, what looked to be note cards in her hand. Good God, her "brief remarks"! Percival's life as a headmaster passed before his eyes. . . .*

## THE WHITE HOUSE WEST WING

### MAY 26 (10:45 A.M.)

"Walk in *my* shoes, Lee. All *you* have to do next month is keep the world thinking your boss is alive. *I* draw double-duty. Keep the White House staff thinking he's alive; the President thinking he's nuts."

All White House staffers but Mrs. Kaltenborn, of course. She was back with a carafe of hot water and a clutch of Red Zinger teabags, the coffee finally having run out. The sealed missive to Otto De Faye had been dispatched via the U.S. Marines, she informed us. One of the dress-blue White House guards would be delivering it any minute. "I'm sure," she added, "Mr. De Faye will be properly impressed."

"Semper Fi," said Strong. "That takes care of *that.*"

Mrs. Kaltenborn mixed two cups of Red Zinger, duly reported that the President hadn't called in thirty minutes, and took her leave.

"McCluskey solved, De Faye solved," said Strong, returning to his desk calendar. "No problems." He sipped his tea and pointed to the calendar with an extended pinky. "Your boss has zilch scheduled in June," he said. "Only a post office ribbon cutting in Boise, Idaho, on the eighth and another in Salisbury, Maryland, on the nineteenth. Both scrubbed."

"Since when?" I asked.

"Or *will* be scrubbed," said Strong, "unless you know a way to cut ribbons by phone hookup." His eyes narrowed. "What's wrong, Lee? Something in your craw? Spit it out."

"Three points," I said. "First, the President's not knowing his Vice President's dead. That still bugs me."

"*Bugs* you?"

"*Surveils* me, bothers me, whatever. I just don't think it's right."

"*Right?* Oh, I see, that's what you want to talk about," replied Strong, looking not at me but at the Presidential seal on his teacup. "Okay, let's talk *right.* Man phones me, four in the morning, says his boss is dead but he doesn't want to report it to the cops. Can I help him out? Get rid of the stiff? Not to worry, I say. Understand now, the man calls *me,* I didn't call *him.* So after—"

"So much for Point One," I said. "Point Two: What do we do if the President isn't renominated?"

Strong's cup and saucer clattered to the floor.

"Let me put it another way," I said, ignoring the commotion. "Suppose the dozen—dozen and a half?—governors you've promised the Vice Presidency, suppose they compare notes?"

"Compare notes?" repeated Strong, staring at the mess that he (and by proximate cause, I) had made on his government heirloom throw rug. "They compare notes all the time." He looked up and through me. "So?"

"So," I said, "if one governor you've promised tells another governor you've promised, then . . . ?"

"Then the second governor will think the first governor's a fool for believing he's wanted or needed on a national ticket," replied Strong. "He'll say to himself, 'The President may have told him that, but he didn't mean it. *I'm* the one he wants and needs as his running mate.' " Strong shook his head. "You know, Lee," he said, "it's when you ask questions like that . . ."

He exhaled, leaned over, and began picking up shards of White House crockery. "Anything else?" he said, gingerly pitching the jagged pieces into a wastebasket.

"Last point," I asked. "The Caribbean Summit. It comes up June twentieth—"

"Phase One," Strong corrected. What about it?"

"Only that it's a major media event," I replied. "Fidel Castro comes to Washington for the first time in over thirty years and Vice President Vandercleve is nowhere to be seen. We can scrub Boise and Salisbury, but how do we finesse that?"

Strong pressed a button. Mrs. Kaltenborn reappeared. "Mrs. K.," he said, "a black cat ran across my desk and made a mess. A tea stain on the rug and they're a bitch to remove. Call housekeeping."

Mrs. Kaltenborn walked across the room and glared down at the rug.

"The Castro visit," said Strong, now shuffling papers on his desk. "Frankly, I hadn't thought about that. It does pose something of a PR dilemma, doesn't it?"

I nodded.

"It'll be interesting," said Regis Strong, "to see how you work your way out of it."


FYI, as all summit buffs know, the Caribbean Summit had been shrewdly timed to benefit the President's campaign for renomination and reelection. Phase One, Castro would visit Washington just before the GOP convention; Phase Two, the President would visit Havana, just before the November election.

Why Castro? Who else was there to summit with? Albania? China was used up; Russia was old hat. Castro was the only world leader left with box-office appeal. Enough to knock the President's opponents off the front page and hype his campaign slogan: KEEP THE GREAT PEACEMAKER IN THE WHITE HOUSE.

Why the Great Peacemaker? Again, the obvious choice. The President's ad agency had conducted a field test of possible themes for the campaign. One possibility was the Great Peacemaker, another was Mr. Compassion. When the results came back, aside from a random variable in Southern California (the Big Wavemaker), peace had the big numbers.

Not that everyone bought the Summit idea. The package included having Fidel address a joint session of Congress. The House approved it in a vote on May 1, but an anti-Castro resolution was up in the Senate, which if passed could embarrass the President on the eve of Castro's arrival in Washington.

The vote would be close. Close enough to keep Strong on the phone, talking for the third time that morning to a swing vote, Senator I. D. Newmark, even as I left his office and headed back to my own for a hard day's session with the Muse. Or so I thought.

# THE VICE PRESIDENT'S PRESS OFFICE

MAR 26 (11:15 A.M.)

★ Carla met me at the door with a fistful of phone memos: a few merely IMPORTANT, some tagged AS SOON AS POSSIBLE, others SOONER THAN POSSIBLE.

The IMPORTANT calls included one from Miriam Little-paugh, informing me that McCluskey was back at his desk, reassuringly dull and sober for the first time in days; another from Sam Andreas, with what Carla said was a "cryptic" message about a "mole" at Sabatino's; and a third from my son, which Carla, with uncharacteristic coyness, chose not to relay.

The ASAP list, with Carla's comments, included Ben Colfax *(Abrasive. Trying to run down facts on Hill about VP's blind* trust.); FBI Director Mize *(Furious at being "stonewalled" by the VP's staff)*; and Otto De Faye *(Apologetic about yesterday's tantrum. Says he now understands perfectly, and will make it up to you with a free shampoo and styling. What does he mean by "now understands," and why should YOU get the freebies when I took the flak?).*

The STP list led off with C. Foster Abel *(Called at 9:35. Says Senate committee hearing "didn't go well for VP," but refused to elaborate over phone.)*; Romana Clay *(Called at 10:30. Agitated. Used language not fit for family memo.)*; and the Second Lady *(Called 11:00. Agitated, furious, abrasive. Reminded me of VP on one of his bad-bear days).*

"Start with the Second Lady," I said. "Call the residence."

"She's not *at* the residence," replied Carla. "She's in the air, somewhere between Barton and Washington. What are you searching for?"

"Another set of worry beads," I said, going through desk drawers. "We've got a rough June ahead. *Found* 'em!" I held up the white-speckled string of beads that saw me through the worst hours of Bully's Pro-Am Golf fiasco. Then, little knowing how soon they'd be put to use: "Why'd she leave so early? She's not due at Barton till tonight."

"What are you talking about?" said Carla. "She's on her way *back* from Barton."

"Back? What went wrong? She's not handing out the diplomas?"

"She *already* handed out the diplomas," said Carla, cocking her head portside. "Also, according to the wires, made a speech, just as I said she would. Pretty fair speech. Not enough to upstage the Vice President's, of course."

"Are we on two tracks again?" I asked. "*What* Vice President's speech?" I lifted a blank page, holding it eye level. "*Here* is the Vice President's Barton Academy speech, as of"—I checked my Swatch—"eleven-forty-five Ante Meridian, Thursday, May twenty-fifth. A *tabula rasa,* as you can see. Close the door gently on leaving, return in two hours, and I'll have something on it to send over to Feinbaum."

Carla cocked her head starboard and looked at me strangely, which is to say, sympathetically, not her standard reaction to inner-office sarcasm.

"Why," I asked, "are you looking at me like that?"

"McCluskey," she replied. "I'm wondering whether whatever he had is contagious. This is"—she checked her ladies Seiko—"eleven-forty-eight Ante Meridian, Friday, May twenty-sixth, Frank. You're one day and three minutes slow. The VP's speech went over to Feinbaum first thing this morning. He rehearsed it, called it in by phone—"

"I repeat: *What* Vice President's speech?"

"*Your* Vice President's speech, Frank," replied Carla. " 'Arise, Young Americans!' remember? The one you left on your desk. . . ."

## EXCERPT, ABC EVENING NEWS WITH HIBBERT WEATHERS

### MAY 26 (6:31 P.M.)

WEATHERS: Vice President Vandercleve was involved in yet another controversy today, this time over alleged remarks he made to the graduating class at Barton Academy, Connecticut. Speaking by phone hookup from his Washington office, the Vice President shocked the administration and faculty of that staid institution by advocating—according to a wire service string correspondent present—redistribution of the nation's wealth and a return by American youth to what he called, quote, the revolutionary spirit, unquote, of the generation of the sixties. Mr. Vandercleve, himself reputed to be one of America's richest men, called for, I quote, power to the people, unquote, through, quote, radical reform, unquote, including heavier taxes for upper-income groups. The Vice President asked, quote, what is property, unquote, citing a French revolutionary's rallying cry, quote, property is theft, unquote. In addition, he used, to the dismay of his hosts, several blunt barnyard expressions to make his points.

Parents of Barton's graduating seniors were said to be livid over the Vice President's remarks, though the graduates themselves gave him a standing ovation when he finished.

Asked for comment, a White House spokesman said the Vice President was speaking on his own behalf and, again I quote, his remarks do not—repeat, do not—reflect the views of the President or the administration, unquote.

A side note: The President's wife was present at the Barton ceremonies and made a little news in her own right. After sharply criticizing the Academy for having an all-male student body and discriminating against women in its hiring practices, the Second Lady said that while those policies were, quote, rooted in the past, unquote, the current national administration—of which her husband is a member—has encouraged those attitudes by—again I quote—a seventeenth-century approach to the role of women in society.

Vice President Vandercleve's Barton speech, as well as his political future this election year, will be the subject of a special edition of Walt Kendall's "NightBeat" on this network later this evening.

Elsewhere, campaigning in Biloxi, Mississippi, Senator Buzz Stanton today charged . . .

No point blaming Carla for my own screw-up because, even if she'd taken time to look over the speech, it seemed like a perfect fit for Operation Avis: guaranteed, like the letters to Steinem and Hewlett, to move the Vice President front and center in the news.

Not that all our co-conspirators were especially pleased with this latest triumph of political image over substance. . . .

SIGNAL: Mr. Lee—

FL: Yes, I know. Mr. Strong on the line.

SIGNAL: That's right, sir.

RS: Lee? Well, I hand it to you, old buddy. You laid in enough coals today to burn through the winter. I just got a call—

FL: Let me—

RS: From guess who? You practically knocked him off the evening news. He delivers a major foreign policy speech in Houston, a speech they've worked on for two weeks, and he gets thirty seconds of air time, while his Vice President gets a minute and a half.

FL: —explain. I was out of the office and there was a mis-understanding about the speech.

RS: Which *(expletive deleted)* speech? His or hers?

FL: Her speech? Oh, yeah. Listen, we have a separate prob-lem there, one that may get out of hand.

RS: Well, the President's convinced your boss is *non com-pos,* so it won't come as too much of a surprise to find out the wife is too. But the word, Lee, listen up, now, the word is, the President's tired of hearing about Vander-cleve. He wants a gag on, a total *(expletive deleted)* gag. No more media.

FL: No media? But the whole idea behind the Operation is to make people think—

RS: That's just the point, Lee. You've got 'em thinking too much. I'm just telling you what the President told me. A gag, a lid. Someway, somehow, you'll just have to keep the thing going without—

FL:     Yeah, well, I'll try, I'll try. But—

RS:     Got to go. President's due at Andrews.


*Transcript, Tape No. 117-A, the President's impromptu news conference on return from Southern campaign swing, 26 May (2015 hours).*

1ST REPORTER:    Mr. President, your opponent Senator STAN-TON says you're DUCKING a second *debate*—

P:     Bait? Can't hear you. The helicopter is—

2ND REPORTER:    Your SPEECH in Houston. Do you expect to TAKE TEXAS?

P:     Raise taxes? No, absolutely not.

3RD REPORTER:    But Vice President Vandercleve said—

P:     Vandercleve dead?

3RD REPORTER:    No, he said—

P:     Sorry, I just can't hear you. The helicopter is—

4TH REPORTER:    What about CISSY Vandercleve's speech? She says your administration is guilty of BLATANT SEXISM.

P:     Take Texas? Yes, I think I will.

3RD REPORTER:    Are you going to TALK to Vice President Vander-cleve about his speech?

2ND REPORTER:    And CISSY Vandercleve's speech?

1ST REPORTER:    Will you DEBATE Stanton?

P:     Well, yes, no. What?

# THE "NIGHTBEAT" GREEN ROOM

## MAY 26 (10:45 P.M.)

Ben Colfax, the Prince of Darkness, was glaring at me. If I'd known *he* was going to be on the show, I'd have turned Kendall down, packed it in for the day, and headed home.

Home? No, grim as the prospect was, I'd rather go up against the Prince at the moment than whatever waited for me back home. How do I explain Tommy's speech being used by the Vice President?

"Tell me, Lee, what's your man up to? And don't hand me any crap."

"What?"

"I said, what's your man up to?" repeated Colfax. "I mean, the attack on Steinem and the music critic I could understand."

"You could?"

"Trying to butter up the right wing to keep from getting dumped, wasn't he?"

I shrugged.

"I thought so," drawing the wrapper off a panatela. "But this caper at Barton"—he worked a straight match out of his coat pocket and struck it, backhand, on the sign directly above him that warned: SMOKING PROHIBITED—$100 FINE FOR VIOLATORS—"this caper at Barton has to be the dumbest political move by a Vice President since . . ."

His voice trailed off. Carla had been against having me go on the Kendall show, but of course I knew better. Walt Kendall was a good interview, I said. ("That's just the point," she replied. *"Too* good.") Still, I just couldn't let the Barton speech hang out there, unexplained. It needed clarification. But with Colfax as my fellow panelist, the question was whether I'd get a chance to clarify.

"You know something, Lee?" Colfax was saying. "I've gone through every Vice President since I've been in this town, all the way back to Nixon, and I can't for the life of me *remember* a dumber political move."

He sat there, sullen eyes doing their number on his cigar, daring the ash to flicker out. Then: *"Nobody* is that dumb, Lee, not even in this administration. Your man's up to something, and I think I know what it is."

"You do?"

"That rumor on Capitol Hill about his blind trust," he said. "Whatever he's hiding"—he sent white billows across the room— "it's bad enough to make him set up a smoke screen, right?"

"What rumor?" I asked, fighting off the fog.

Colfax laughed, more precisely, sneered.

"Makeup?" asked a cherubic studio gofer who suddenly appeared at the door. She pointed to a wall clock above the Prince's noncherubic head. "Mr. Kendall wants you on set at eleven-fifteen."

"Don't use cosmetics," said Colfax. He pointed toward me. *"That's* your man, right there."

*Excerpt, "NightBeat," with host Walt Kendall, ABC-TV, May 26*

KENDALL: Then what you're saying is, the Vice President didn't tell the graduating class at Barton that he favors redistribution of wealth and higher taxes?

LEE: I said it at the top of the show, and I'll repeat it, Walt. In all the years I've worked for Bully Vandercleve, he never—I say, never—favored any of those things.

KENDALL: But according to the news report—

LEE: Are we talking about what the Vice President stands for or about news reports?

KENDALL: Are you claiming he was quoted out of context? Is that it?

LEE: Exactly. Quoted out of context, and not for the first time. It's an old story, the press corps ganging up on a public figure, distorting what he says. You did it to Nixon, you did it to Carter, you did it to Reagan, you did it to Gary Hart, you did it to—

COLFAX: Now wait just a damn minute. I've been here, patiently waiting my turn, but I don't have to listen to a hired political gun bashing the media—

LEE: See, Walt? Just what I said. A gang-up. That's why the Vice President isn't here tonight. He's taken enough abuse from the press corps in one day, so why let you and your friend Colfax here gang up on him, two to one?

KENDALL: Is that your opinion, Frank, or the Vice President's? I mean, that the media is—

LEE: I'm the press secretary, Walt. I speak for the Vice President.

### VANDERCLEVE ASSAILS PRESS FOR SPEECH "DISTORTION"

*—Headline, page one,
the* Los Angeles Times, *May 27*


FYI, the network's phone lines in New York and Washington were tied up a good two hours after the show, eight out of ten viewers calling to protest the way the news media was ganging up on the Vice President.

### SURVEY OF PUBLIC OPINION SAMPLING OF 600 PHONE INTERVIEWEES (MAY 27–30)

QUESTION: *Do you believe Vice President Vandercleve favors the redistribution of wealth, higher taxes, or anything else the news media says he said at Barton Academy?*

| | |
|---|---|
| Yes | 3% |
| No | 66% |
| I wouldn't believe the news media under any circumstances | 15% |
| Undecided | 12% |
| Who is Vice President Vandercleve? | 4% |

The really interesting item in the poll was that last number. A Vice President known by 96 percent of the American people! Bully now had the highest name ID of any Vice President in twenty years. A ten-strike, thanks to the "NightBeat" interview. And the odd thing is that I hadn't thought of using the old out-of-context excuse until Kendall reminded me of all the mileage we got out of taking on Steinem and that rock critic. Improv, as Feinbaum would say, improv. Or as my mentor, Phil Madvig, once put it: Rule Number 10—*Good news, get it out; bad news, maim the messenger.*

Not that my "NightBeat" performance was an unmitigated triumph. I'd ticked off the Prince of Darkness, never a good idea for a political flack in an election year, whether his candidate is living or dead.

Unfortunately, media bashing couldn't solve my credibility crisis back home. How could I explain the plagiarizing of Tommy's speech by the Vice President? I put the inevitable off as long as possible, closing the Press Club bar at 1:00 A.M., then taking the 14th Street bridge into Northern Virginia. Even at that hour there might be a traffic jam that would give me more time to think.

The 14th Street bridge seldom disappoints. A road-repair crew had tied up two lanes and a three-car fender bender had blocked another. I turned on my car radio, listened to Joe Bristle ("The King of Insult FM") berate a few insomniac callers, then opted for silence to consider my options. I could tell them I'd been drugged. Or that the Vice President had been seized by terrorists and made the speech at gunpoint. Or that there were national security reasons I couldn't discuss.

I could see the first two selling to the supermarket tabloid set (UFO CREATURES DRUG VP AIDE), but not to skeptics like my wife and son. The third option had a shot, however. Not that it made any more sense than the other two, but as an all-purpose conversation-stopper, national security has no peer. At least not in Washington.

The traffic jam broke. I headed across the bridge, down Shirley Highway. Before I knew it, I was pulling into my garage, primed to take the offensive if one or both met me at the door. National security. It just might work. . . .

*Excerpt, Tape No. 106-T, conversation in family room of Frank Lee's residence, inc. Frank Lee, Maureen Lee, Thomas S. Lee, 27 May (0215 hours).*

FL:      All right, settle down. Before you say anything at all, hear me out.

ML:      We're waiting.

TL:      Waiting.

FL:      Fine, but you better sit down first.

ML:      Okay, we're sitting down.

FL:      Now what I'm about to tell you involves a crisis of the first magnitude at the highest level of American government. The future of the Free World is—

TL:      Pop, I certainly hope you're not going to hand us the usual government *(expletive deleted)* about national security.

FL:      Certainly not. What gave you that idea? What I'm about to say is—

ML:      We're waiting.

FL:     What I'm about to say is—

TL:     Waiting.

FL:     The Vice President is dead.

**MEMORANDUM**

## OFFICE OF THE VICE PRESIDENT
### WASHINGTON

CODE AMBER:
SHRED DATE   June 30.

**DATE:**   MAY 29
**TO:**   CARLA BRAUNSCHWEIG
**FROM:**   FRANK LEE
**SUBJECT:**  OPERATION AVIS

1. Be advised that the number total on the Need to Know list should be revised upward, from 36 to 38.

2. As per Executive Order 43, re special funding of said Operation, please purchase from Computers-R-Us one (1) Ultra Speed Laser Printer, along with (1) Deluxe Issue Super Drive Modem, to be delivered ASAP to Mr. Thomas S. Lee, 6632 Canterbury Road, Falls Church, VA. No card or questions needed.

SEGMENT THREE

## A Brokered Convention for GOP?

*—Headline,* Washington Post, *May 31*

### Election Roundup

The Southern primaries had been touted as the place where the President would finally put Buzz Stanton's presidential challenge to rest, but nothing of the sort happened.

With 1,175 convention votes needed to nominate, the tally coming out of Grits Tuesday is 755 for the

President, 738 for Senator Stanton, and—in an interesting development—16 for Vice President Vandercleve, picked up as a result of write-in votes in Florida, Georgia, Louisiana, and Texas.

On the Democratic side, Southern primary voters winnowed the presidential field down to a manageable nine, with seven weeks to go until the party convention in Orlando. . . .

*—Excerpt,* USA Today, *May 31*

*"I like what Bully Vandercleve's saying. I don't always understand what it is, but at least he's saying something."*
*—Louisiana Republican, replying to pollster's postprimary question on why he wrote in Vice President Vandercleve's name on the Presidential ballot.*

## THE VICE PRESIDENT'S PRESS OFFICE

MAY 31 (9:30 A.M.)

Carla, asking questions:
"Have you heard about the Second Lady's speaking schedule for the next two weeks? What do you make of those write-ins?"

No comment, no comment. Yes, the Second Lady had told (warned?) me about her upcoming speeches, and I'd heard all I wanted to hear about those write-ins from Regis Strong, at 8:00 A.M. The President, he said, was imperially pissed. And that was before he'd seen the Sage column in the *Post.* . . .

# VANDERCLEVE'S GAME PLAN
## By
## Jeremiah Sage

"There is more here," as Talleyrand shrewdly remarked to Louis XVIII on hearing of Bonaparte's escape from Elba, "than meets the eye." Talleyrand was right, of course, and the same can be said of those who now perceive Vice President Vandercleve's recent burst of political activity as an ingenious campaign to preclude his being dumped from this year's Republican ticket.

To some obtuse observers, Vandercleve's new-found prominence after years of quiescent vice presidential servitude is regarded as merely the last gasp of a once-promising national leader in the twilight of his career. But to paraphrase the Duke of Wellington's stinging riposte on one famous occasion, if they believe that, sir, they can believe anything.

Consider, if you will, the sheer magnitude, not to say brilliance, of the Vandercleve game plan. In little more than a fortnight he has rallied to his side the ever-puissant antimedia, conservative wing of his party, while at the same time, in the most provocative commencement address since John F. Kennedy addressed the Notre Dame graduating class in the early sixties, boldly reaching out to stir the liberal imagination of America's young, its powerless, its middle-class masses yearning to be free. . . .

Indeed, one may wonder whether a politically enfeebled President can now afford the luxury of replacing Bully Vandercleve as his running mate; assuming, of course, that the incumbent himself is renominated at the GOP convention. And more: one might wonder whether a Vice President who three times tried and failed to gain his party's presidential nomination has not at long last come into his own, with a game plan that would make him the logical compromise candidate should that convention deadlock. . . .

★ 153 ★

*Transcript, Tape No. 276-C, telephone conversation be-*
*tween Frank Lee, press secretary to the Vice President, and*
*Romana Clay, 31 May (0945 hours).*

FL:   Romie! Back from the sunny South—

RC:   Have you seen Sage's column?

FL:   Yeah.

RC:   Well, you've done it, Lee, you've finally done it. There are
      three, maybe four, columnists in this town whose every word
      is read by the network brass and taken as gospel. The Sage
      column—

FL:   Is what we want, right? A month to go, we can practically
      coast home. Then, the July First announcement—

RC:   Coast? I just came out of a session with my bureau chief. He
      got a call this morning from New York. The Barton speech,
      the write-in votes, now the Sage column—you know what
      they want?

FL:   Haven't the foggiest.

RC:   They say Vandercleve's fight to stay on the ticket is the
      hottest political story going. So they want their ace Washing-
      ton correspondent—the one with entrée to high places, you
      know?—to live up to her star billing. Not to mention her
      seven-figure salary.

FL:   Oh? Putting somebody on the spot, huh?

RC:   That's me they talking about, Lee. They're pulling me off the
      campaign to work full time on a special segment for the
      evening news. More than just an interview, they want the
      whole schmeer. A political profile. Working title—

FL:   Profile?

RC:   "A Day in the Life of Bully Vandercleve."


Carla at the door again, asking questions:
"I don't suppose you ever got back to Foster Abel, did you?"

"You're right, I didn't."

"You know he's testifying today?"

"Slipped my mind."

"Yes, well the chief counsel of the Committee he's testifying before is on the line. You care to talk to him?"

"No, but I will. What's his name?"

"Cruiser, something like that."

"Put him on."


*Transcript, Tape No. 277-A, telephone conversation between Frank Lee, press secretary to the Vice President, and Ellis Cruse, chief counsel for the Senate Committee on Investment Fraud, 31 May (0955 hours).*

FL: Mr. Cruiser, Frank Lee. What can I do for you?

EC: Cruse. Ellis Cruse, Mr. Lee, chief counsel for the Stanton Committee. And before we get started, it's my duty to notify you that our conversation is being recorded.

FL: Bugged?

EC: No, recorded. As you know, the Committee has the authority—

FL: Now wait just a *(expletive deleted)* minute, Mr. Cruse. I'm press secretary to the Vice President of the United States and I'm not accustomed to having my phone conversations recorded.

EC: Mr. Lee, we can argue about that and I can get the necessary papers to send two investigators down to your office to question you. But I assure you, sir, we have the legal right—

FL: Two investigators to question me? About what?

EC: For the record, Mr. Lee, we're not interested in questioning you, but the Vice President. I'm calling at the specific direction of Senator Stanton—

FL: Question the Vice President? Why?

EC:   Are you aware, Mr. Lee, that Mr. C. Foster Abel appeared before the committee in open session this morning?

FL:   Abel?

EC:   Yes, and are you—have you been apprised—of the nature of his testimony?

FL:   What he said?

EC:   More to the point, Mr. Lee, what he didn't say. Asked about his role as executor of the Vice President's blind trust, he took the Fifth Amendment no fewer than thirty-six times.

FL:   Abel took the Fifth?

EC:   Three-score times, on the advice of his counsel—who, I might add, is the most arrogant *(expletive deleted)* I have ever had the good fortune to question, live and on camera.

FL:   Good fortune?

EC:   Yes, if it hadn't been for Abel's lawyer, all we'd have on the network tonight was ten seconds of him taking the Fifth, but as it is we have quite a show. But back to the purpose of my call. We have, you know, a delicate situation here, because the Committee would prefer to get the information it wants from Mr. Abel rather than the Vice President.

FL:   Information about what?

EC:   Mr. Lee, let's not be coy. I was told by Mr. McCluskey that you were the party to speak to about the possibility of questioning the Vice President under oath—

FL:   Coy, me? Listen, Cruse, I don't know what Stanton thinks he's up to—

EC:   I sense, Mr. Lee, by the tone of your voice—

FL:   —but regardless of what Foster Abel said or didn't say, there is no chance, none at all, that Vice President Vandercleve, a member of the executive branch, will consent to being questioned by a Senate committee.

EC:   Separation of powers, is that what you're claiming? Or executive privilege? There's a fine constitutional point here, Mr. Lee—

FL:   The answer is no, period. Tell Senator Stanton the Vice President has more important things to do.


Coming on pretty strong maybe, but my idea was to throttle that monster before it crawled out of its cave. Bully testify? About what? Twenty-four hours later I found out, when, playing one of Carla's hunches, I finally got around to a one-on-one with Max Mize. Not over the phone, however. At his office in the J. Edgar Hoover Building where, he said, we could talk freely, with no chance of being bugged.


*Excerpt of transcript, Tape No. 111-Z, meeting between FBI Director Maximilian M. Mize and Frank Lee, press secretary to the Vice-President, J. Edgar Hoover Building, 1 June (1115 hours).*

MMM:  So that there be no misapprehension on your part, Mr. Lee, I am sorely disappointed that the Vice President has preemptively dismissed numerous requests on my part to interface on matters of mutual interest. Is my meaning manifest?

FL:   You're *(expletive deleted)* off because the Vice President hasn't returned your calls?

MMM:  Quite. May I presume—pure conjecture on my part—that his reluctance to talk to me is related to certain unresolved questions about his fiduciary relationship with C. Foster Abel?

FL:   Abel? You know something about that situation?

MMM:  Indeed I do. Enough so that the embarrassment inflicted on Mr. Abel yesterday might have been avoided had the Vice President not rejected my telephonic overtures.

FL:     Oh?

MMM:    But time being of the essence—with the proviso that I
        still wish to speak to your principal—let me pursue the
        matter with you. I presume, Mr. Lee, that you're author-
        ized to intake confidential data on the Vice President's
        behalf?

FL:     I'm what?

MMM:    Cleared.

FL:     Mr. Mize, talking to me is as good as talking to Vice
        President Vandercleve.

MMM:    Indeed. Understand then that the data I am about to im-
        part, though not classified, is highly sensitive: It appears
        that over an extended time frame the Vice President's
        friend has disseminated advance information regarding no
        fewer than half a dozen corporate mergers and acquisi-
        tions . . .

FL:     So?

MMM:    . . . to a few favored clients. Unfortunately, Mr. Abel was
        a board member, as well as legal counsel, for the affected
        business entities, which made his actions, to say the least,
        indiscreet. Do you follow my meaning?

FL:     Not yet.

MMM:    Insider trading, Mr. Lee, insider training. A veritable *(ex-
        pletive deleted)* potful of money has changed hands, and
        that, precisely, is what the Senate Committee is looking
        into.

FL:     Right. So tell me, what does all this have to do with Vice
        President Vandercleve? In plain English.

MMM:    Plain English? He was one of Abel's preferred clients to the
        tune of ten mil.

FL:   Bully Vandercleve involved in a stock swindle? You've got to be—

MMM:  Swindle? An inappropriate term in this case, Mr. Lee. Scam is more like it.

FL:   But why—

MMM:  My initial reaction precisely. Why would one of the richest men in America participate in a scam involving a mere ten million dollars? It's one of the questions I hope to pursue with your principal.

FL:   And you're sure of your information?

MMM:  I have unimpeachable sources on the Hill.

FL:   I can believe that, but the Vice President has a blind trust—

MMM:  Mr. Lee, my experience is that blind trusts in Washington retain seeing-eye dogs. That, at least, is what Senator Stanton—

FL:   Stanton. How much does he know?

MMM:  About the Vice President's involvement? Nothing specific as yet, though my Hill informants tell me that his investigators are in hot pursuit. So much for the downside.

FL:   There's an upside?

MMM:  Affirmative. That sensitive matter I referred to earlier. According to certain files in my possession—personal, not Bureau files, understand—Senator Stanton himself has certain, shall I say, skeletons in his portmanteau.

FL:   Oh? And, uh, does Senator Stanton know about your files?

MMM:  Negative. But he will, should the need and opportunity arise.

FL:   I see. Well, then, would you, ah, mind sharing—

★ 159 ★

MMM: Negative. Much as I respect your exalted position, Mr. Lee, I will impart this information to no one but Vice President Vandercleve personally.

FL: A hint maybe?

MMM: Only that it involves specific indiscretions in the Senator's past relating to sexual—ah—encounters.

FL: Of the third kind?

MMM: Nothing quite that good. But sufficient, I daresay, to give a man with presidential ambitions serious pause before proceeding along his present line of inquiry. Now, as to my purpose in making this data available to the Vice President—

FL: Only the Vice President? What about the White House?

MMM: Negative. The White House, given the current political situation, would utilize the files not so much to aid the Vice President as to discredit the Senator. And aiding the Vice President is my sole purpose here, Mr. Lee. You understand that, of course.

FL: Of course.

MMM: Have you heard, Mr. Lee—more to the point, has the Vice President heard—of my imminent plans to retire from the public sector?

FL: Retire? Oh, yeah. End of the year, right? I did read something about that. You're planning to—

MMM: Establish and operate a foundation, Mr. Lee, a vast educational center. The largest, most modern facility for the training of law-enforcement officers in in the world. I have a dream, Mr. Lee, a state-of-the-art dream. I envision, in some appropriate locale—La Jolla, Palm Springs—one vast enterprise dedicated solely to the enhancement of the American—

FL:     And this dream of yours, Mr. Mize, exactly, uh, how much—

MMM:   Oh, I'd say ten mil for seed money. Twenty, thirty as the project gets legs.

FL:     Twenty, thirty?

MMM:   Thirty, tops.

FL:     I'll get back to you.

MMM:   By all means, Mr. Lee, by all expeditious means.


I'll say this about Bully, for a dead Vice President he was full of surprises.

After my session with Mize I headed back to the office by way of the National Press Club bar, both to get in touch with the native tongue and to think things through.

*Why did he do it?* It wasn't the paltry ten million, I knew that. So why would the richest politician in America get involved in a Wall Street scam? Back to Basic Megalomania, 101: a man born to power and influence gets stuck in a job without power or influence. Along comes an old friend with a shrewd business proposition, a high-risk gamble . . .

Right. For Bully, insider trading was no more than a game to relieve the boredom of Vice Presidential days, like one of those $5,000-a-hole side wagers he'd make at Burning Tree. And maybe something else. In his third-generational way he was carrying on a family tradition by getting an edge on the rest of the world. Wasn't manipulation and market-rigging how old Otis B. Vandercleve first made the family fortune, back in the 1890s? Of course, in those days it wasn't considered illegal, or if it was, the law could be bought off.

Bully probably figured that if he did get caught he could buy his way out of trouble the way Granddaddy did. More likely he didn't figure to get caught dabbling on Wall Street, any more than he'd get caught dabbling with Romana Clay. That was why, no doubt about it. Screwing Romie and screwing Wall Street were just two sides of the same imperial coin.

### SECOND LADY LAUNCHES NATIONAL "ANTIPOLLUTION CRUSADE"
### SAYS WHITE HOUSE "SPURNS SERIOUS ISSUE"

*—Headline,* Atlanta Constitution, *page 2, over
story re Cissy Vandercleve's speech before
the Georgia State Society to Close the
Ozone Hole, June 2.*

*Transcript, Tape No. 259-C, complete, unedited telephone
conversation between Regis Strong, WH chief of staff, and Frank
Lee, press secretary to the Vice President 2 June (0858 hours).*

RS: Lee?

FL: I know.

Twenty-eight days to go, twenty-nine balls in the air. Still, I could have finessed the Stanton Committee if it hadn't been for that oddball in the lot: How could I have filed and forgotten, of all co-conspirators, The Man of a Thousand Voices?

## THE HANDYMEN'S SAFE-HOUSE
### JUNE 2 (11:30 P.M.)

*Feinbaum hadn't had this much fun since he'd played Caesar's Palace with Jackie Mason. Fresh country air, gourmet deli and Szechuan, and five massages a day (not including matinees)—and all for God and country. So the President wanted* the KGB disinformed, did he? Make them think the Vice President is in Washington when he's really on a secret mission? Relax, bubala. Feinbaum's on the case.

Nightcap time and Helga had the radio on, playing the Joe Bristle call-in show. She liked listening to the show because Bristle, the host, confirmed her low opinion of American men as rude, crude, insulting louts. There were two topics under discussion, typical call-in fare. The first was whether cats make better housepets than dogs; the second, whether Bully Vandercleve should be dumped from the Republican ticket. Bristle, as usual, took both sides of each argument, depending on how his caller felt.

"I guess you do like dogs," he was telling a young housewife named Nell. "Prob'ly eat Alpo, right? Arf-arf!" He clicked her off, chuckled at his little insult, and took the next call. It was a cab driver named E. Ray, to say that he was a great fan of the Vice President, and thought he ought to be kept on the ticket.

"The Dilettante Veep?" said Bristle. "Talk about dogs! Hey, gimme a break. I'd like to hear one good reason why that no-talent, lightweight oughta be one heartbeat away from—"

"Now hold on, Joe, you're talkin' about the Vice President of our country," said the caller. "I mean, show a little respect. We're all Americans and—"

"Who the hell are you to lecture me about patriotism?" Bristle broke in. "I took two big ones at DaNang, mister, while you were still pushing kiddie cars. I say Vandercleve is a no-talent dilettante, and oughta be dumped. Thanks for calling." He cut E. Ray off in midreply and broke for a commercial.

Feinbaum had heard enough. He nudged past Helga and snatched up the phone.

Headline and excerpt of story, page 1, "Style" section, *Washington Post,* June 3:

## VEEP AND TALK-SHOW HOST
## IN LATE-NIGHT BARBFEST
### by
### Jamie Paige

Joe Bristle earned his reputation as a talk-show host the hard-nosed way, by perfecting an equal-opportunity radio style that manages to offend everyone, regardless of race, creed, gender, or political persuasion. But last night, the man who calls himself "The King of Insult FM" met his match in what will go down as the most abrasive exchange between a politician and a TV-radio personality since then-Vice President George Bush and CBS's Dan Rather had at it back in 1988.

One of Bristle's topics in the early segment of this WOW-FM show was whether Bully Vandercleve should be dumped from the Republican ticket this fall. A caller had just registered his support for the Vice President, leading the program host to put Vandercleve down as, variously, a dog, a "no-talent lightweight," and "a Dilettante Veep."

Nothing surprising there. Just standard Bristle-talk, calculated to get his listeners' blood boiling. What happened next, however, came as a jolt in the night, not only to the show's sizable audience but its always-cocksure host.

It was none other than the Vice President himself, calling in to protest Bristle's "harebrained" commentary and, in a clear reversal of roles, to put the show's host down as a "no-talent mike jockey" who ought to have his "mouth washed out with lye, the way you talk to people."

Vandercleve's call to the station came, according to the program log, at 11:37. The exchange between Bristle and his VIP caller went on for forty-five minutes, the topic of conversation ranging from Vandercleve's view of the upcoming Caribbean Summit ("having Castro to the White House is fine, as long as you hide the good silver") to his preference for cats over dogs as household pets ("Cats have more class. Have you ever seen a cat owner with a pooperscooper?").

Recent weeks have seen the usually reserved Vice President lighten up his public image, in a clear attempt, according to political observers, to win renomination at the Republican convention in Anaheim next month. . . .

## THE PRESS SECRETARY'S FAMILY ROOM
### JUNE 3 (7:15 A.M.)

"You're not just saying that, are you? You really think it came off okay?"

"Not just okay, son, it was the most brilliant valedictory address I've ever heard. Starting with that line about having a speech prepared for the occasion but—how does it go?"

" 'Un mot de—' "

"In English."

" 'A word from the heart is worth ten thousand from a pen.' Rousseau. Actually, it lost something in translation."

The phone rang and Mo caught it.

"Frank, it's Signal."

"Yeah, but what it lost in translation it made up in—"

"Regis Strong, I think."

The second line rang.

"—sincerity."

"Romana Clay on the other line."

"Tell her I've got another call."

I gave our new graduate a paternal chuck under the chin and headed for the phone.

"She says she'll hold."

Strong and Clay, back to back. Something told me Operation Avis had hit the wall.

## LINE 1

SIGNAL:   Mr. Lee, Mr. Strong.

RS:       Have you seen the *Post?*

FL:       No, why? Cissy's made another speech?

RS:       Worse than that. Feinbaum's made another call.

## LINE 2

FL:       Romie, what's up?

RC:       You've seen the *Post?*

FL:       No, but—

RC:       My story, up to now, Lee, has been that the Vice President isn't giving interviews. What do I tell my bureau chief this morning?

## THE VICE PRESIDENT'S PRESS OFFICE

### JUNE 3 (9:10 A.M.)

Carla, on the intercom.

"A call from the Committee. Guess who's *waiting* to talk to you?"

"Cruse again? Tell him to—"

"Not Cruse, his boss," she said. "I think you'd better take it."

Cruse's boss. I looked at the calendar. Twenty-seven days to go. No way to keep him on hold.

*Transcript, Tape No. 249-B, telephone conversation between Frank Lee, press secretary to the Vice President, and Senator B. J. (Buzz) Stanton, 3 June (0915 hours).*

FL: Good morning, Sena—

BJS: Mr. Lee, when a duly elected United States Senator places a call to the Vice President of the United States, he expects to talk to the Vice President, not some *(expletive deleted)* flunky. Now what is this *(expletive deleted)* you gave my counsel yesterday about your boss being too busy to talk to my Committee?

FL: Senator, as I understand the principle of separation of powers—

BJS: Are you a constitutional lawyer?

FL: No.

BJS: So much for that. And so much for the Vice President's taxing schedule. He's too busy to talk to a Senate Committee, but finds time to *(expletive deleted)* around on a radio talk show at all hours of the night.

FL: Senator, let me say that reports of the Vice President being on the radio—

BJS: Okay, we've tried it the nice way—

FL: —were greatly exaggerated.

BJS: —but nice didn't get the job done. So now we do it my way. As of this morning the wheels go in motion to subpoena the Vice President—

FL: Subpoena?

BJS:  —to appear before our Committee on a day certain, there to testify about his knowledge of specific stock transactions—

FL:   Senator, what do you mean, wheels in motion?

BJS:  —involving the executor of his blind trust, C. Foster Abel. I mean, Mr. Lee, we're going to court, if necessary, to get this process moving. That should give the Vice President—are you taking this down?—five, ten days at the most, to decide how he wants it, nice or nasty.

## THE WHITE HOUSE WEST WING

### JUNE 3 (9:45 A.M.)

"Feinbaum is headed west." Strong checked his Rolex. "Should be getting massaged over the Grand Canyon about now."

"Helga went with him?"

"The cook, too," said Strong. "Don't think it doesn't tick Deutsch off. Finding good help for safe-houses isn't easy these days." He studied his fingernails. "The way I see it, Lee, what happened last night was your fault, nobody else's."

"*My* fault? How does that figure?"

Strong shrugged. "Process of elimination," he said. "It wasn't mine, it wasn't Mrs. Kaltenborn's, and it sure as hell wasn't the President's. Know where the old man is right now? Bethesda Naval Hospital, popping diuretics. The press thinks it's a routine checkup, but when he looked at the *Post* this morning—"

The intercom buzzed.

"Bledsoe calling from the Hill," said Mrs. Kaltenborn (who had yet to offer me a cup of coffee; a telltale sign that I'd moved from the palmière to the shit list.)

"If it's another head count, let it ride," said Strong into the squawk box. "I've had enough for the week."

Sid Bledsoe was head of the White House lobbying operation on Capitol Hill. For two straight weeks he and Strong had been hustling Senate votes against the anti-Castro resolution, due to reach the floor June 15. Just about the time Stanton's subpoena reached the Vice President's office.

"You know what that sonofabitch has in mind, of course," said Strong, after I told him about Stanton's threat. "He wants to haul your boss before his committee the last part of June, to steal the headlines from our Castro visit."

"I've still got a problem there," I said. "How do we explain the Vice President's absence from the biggest diplomatic bash of the decade?"

"You've got a bigger problem than that," said Strong. "The head count on the anti-Castro resolution is too close for comfort."

"Since when," I asked, "did that become *my* problem?"

He slipped open a desk drawer and pulled out a slim blue volume: *The United States Constitution: Text with Analytical Index.* " 'Article One, Section Three, Paragraph Four,' " he read, displaying a hitherto unrevealed reverence for the Word. " 'The Vice President of the United States shall be President of the Senate, but shall have no Vote'—emphasis supplied here, Lee—*'unless they be equally divided.' "* He leaned across the desk to point the passage out. "Here," he added. "See for yourself."

" *'Equally divided,' "* I read. "A tie vote."

"Fair translation," replied Strong. "Except for being available when a President dies, the only place a Vice President *has* to be is in the Senate in case of a tie." He drew a cheroot from his coat pocket and peeled the wrapper. "Think about it."

"I'm thinking," I said. "Stanton, Castro, all coming together. It's a sign that maybe—"

"Wrong-think," snapped Strong. "You make that announcement now and it blows the nomination. Not only do we have to pick a new Vice President before the convention, but it blitzes our summit."

The intercom buzzed.

"A call from Bethesda," said Mrs. Kaltenborn. "The President's been discharged and he's on his way back."

"Check," replied Strong. Then, to me: "I was saying?"

"Announcing the Vice President's death would blitz the summit."

"Oh, yeah, right," said Strong. "We can't play pat-the-fanny with Castro while flags are flying half-mast." He lit his cigar and blew three perfect rings. "Unseemly, you know?"

*Transcript, Tape No. 324-Y, telephone conversation between Frank Lee, press secretary to the Vice President, and Regis Strong, WH chief of staff, 3 June (1045 hours).*

FL: I think I've got the answer to our problem.

RS: Listening.

FL: We just make sure there's no tie vote.

RS: Make sure that's no tie vote? Now why didn't I think of that? Lee, we're not fixing a basketball game. There's no point spread to a Senate vote.

FL: You're sure?

RS: Sure I'm sure. The only way to guarantee no tie is—hmm—I see where you're coming from. Not bad. In fact, it has a certain Machiavellian charm. We throw the vote, right? Untwist the arms we've twisted, let the right-wing wackos have their way. Lose by ten or twenty votes, some comfortable margin like that.

FL: Which solves the problem.

RS: Solves your problem, not mine. The State Department's promised Castro the Gold Card treatment, Lee. Room with a view, White House soirée, trip to Disney World, speech on Capitol Hill. The whole summit package, first-class.

FL:   Understood, but—

RS:   Then, last minute, the Senate passes a resolution calling him a Commie sleazeball not fit to speak to Congress. That's a kick in the *(expletive deleted)*, Lee. Not the vibes we're looking for.

FL:   Maybe not, but the alternative—

RS:   There's no alternative, Lee. This summit has to go off, no hitches. The President comes out as a candidate for the Nobel, the Great Peacemaker of the Caribbean Basin. *¿Entiende, amigo?* Take it back to the drawing board.


FYI, the FBI director's proposition did pass through my mind as a way to finesse the Stanton subpoena. I could have called Cissy (somewhere in Oregon, according to news reports, denouncing fur trappers) and she'd have given me a green light to cut a deal. Why not? Underwriting foundations was a Vandercleve hobby and the money involved was a fraction of what Bully had been willing to lay out for an NFL franchise back in the eighties.

Ten, twenty, thirty mil? We could have done it. Easy. But would Bully have wanted it that way? He despised Buzz Stanton, but pulling something out of a man's past—whatever dirty pictures Mize might have had in his file—wasn't Bully's style: *Noblesse oblige.* Cuckold a friend, maybe; but don't screw with his family skeletons.

And yet . . . *If the client knew what was good for him, he wouldn't need a PR man in the first place.* Madvig's Rule No. 2. I reached for the phone.


*Excerpt of transcript, Tape No. 163-X, telephone conversation between Frank Lee, press secretary to the Vice President, and Senator B. J. Stanton, 3 June (1350 hours).*

BJS: Yes, well tell Bully—uh—the Vice President—tell him I appreciate his having you call. But—uh—you're sure Mize didn't give any hint of what he might have in those files?

FL: No, because the Vice President cut the *(expletive deleted)* off as soon as he heard what he was up to. Told him flat-out that he not only didn't care to deal with him but didn't even want to know—

BJS: Yes, of course. But you know, I wonder—uh—did Mize give him any idea where he might have heard we were looking into the—uh—Vice President's affairs?

FL: Well, Senator, since you ask, yes. Mize said he had inside sources. Somebody on the your staff. Didn't say who, but you know how the *(expletive deleted)* operates.

BJS: Hmmm . . . somebody on my staff. That's good to know. But getting back to those files, whatever Mize has, I'm sure it doesn't amount—

FL: Exactly what the Vice President told me. Still, he was pretty upset at what Mize was trying to pull and wanted you to know.

BJS: And I appreciate it. Indeed I do. Tell Bully—the Vice President—tell him I—uh—I owe him one.

**KEEP BULLY VEEP!**
—*Bumper sticker seen on East Coast highway*

**BULLY FOR PREZ!**
—*Bumper sticker seen on West Coast highway*

# THE PRESS SECRETARY'S FAMILY ROOM
## JUNE 4 (8:45 A.M.)

*With Mo, over breakfast . . .*

"You haven't asked for it lately, but would you like my advice?"

"As a wife or a Democrat?"

"As your lawyer."

"Not as a wife?"

"Okay, as a wife, too. The way I see it, you got into what you choose to call 'the Operation' with the best of intentions—"

"I did?"

"To protect your boss's reputation. Then one thing led to another—"

"Is this advice or your speech to the jury?"

"My jury speech comes after I finally add up the laws you've broken. First, impersonating a Vice President."

"That was Feinbaum. All I did was aid and abet."

"Then, forgery—"

"The Autopen did that. I was only a bystander."

"But not an innocent one. Then, illegal use of the mails."

"I used Federal Express."

"All of which comes to—with a sympathetic Republican judge—six months to a year, suspended."

"What about the Stanton problem?"

"That's one I overlooked. Misleading a Senate committee, contempt of Congress—but you're not dug into that hole yet, are you? Which brings me to the big picture as *I* see it."

"And that is . . . ?"

"You've done all you can, Frank—given Bully Vandercleve your best shot. Go down to the office tomorrow and—do you really want to hear this?"

"From my lawyer or my wife?"

"From your lawyer, cut your losses; from your wife, tell the truth."

## THE VICE PRESIDENT'S PRESS OFFICE

### JUNE 5 (9:02 A.M.)

Carla was in midsummer form, glowing from a weekend at the beach. She entered bearing messages, along with an interview tally.

"Total requests for interviews with Vice President Vandercleve, as of this morning, one thousand four hundred and fifty-six. Up three hundred forty-five since last Monday. All on terminal hold." She glanced up from her notebook. "You have an odd look on your face," she said. "What's up?"

"Who's on my call-back list?" I said.

"The usual—Colfax, Clay, McCluskey—"

"Colfax," I said. "Get him on the line."

*Transcript, Tape No. 293-X, telephone conversation between Frank Lee, press secretary to the Vice President, and Ben Colfax, syndicated columnist-commentator, 5 June (0905 hours).*

FL:  Ben? You called?

BC:  And called and called. I remember a time, Lee, in the days your boss was running for President, when I couldn't get you off the line. Now I can't get you on it. I've phoned a dozen times—

FL:  What do you want to know, Ben? About Abel? The story behind the Joe Bristle call-in?

BC: That's two out of six. I want answers, Lee, my readers want answers. What game's your man playing? Is he footing the bill on those Draft Bully clubs around the country? And don't hand me any *(expletive deleted)* about their being spontaneous. What about his wife? Flying around, shaking cages. Answers, Lee, answers. No *(expletive deleted)* either. The truth.

FL: The truth, Ben, is there's a single answer to all your questions. One simple answer. You sitting down?

BC: This better be good.

FL: The truth, Ben—

BC: Yeah?

FL: The truth is—

BC: I'm waiting.

FL: Bully Vandercleve is dead, Ben.

BC: *(Inaudible)*

FL: Colfax? You still there?

BC: Yes, I'm still here, Lee, and believe me, you two-faced *(expletive deleted),* you'll regret this. And whatever it is you and your boss are covering up—whatever—I'll track it down. I'll expose it if it's the last *(expletive deleted)* thing I do.

FL: No, Ben, really. It's the truth. The Vice President is—Ben? Colfax?

So much for truth as a PR ploy in Washington.
I buzzed Carla.
"Who's next?" she asked. "Clay or McCluskey?"
"Neither," I said. "Contact Signal. I want London. Phil Madvig, Esquire, at the Savoy. Either there or Buckingham Palace."

He was a trifle more stooped, and the years since I'd last seen him had brought a touch of gravel to his voice, but he was still the old mentor, the Silver Fox of political public relations, master of the superficial.

When I'd called, he'd dropped everything. "I was prepping Charles for another cameo appearance with Monty Python," he told me on the way into the city from Dulles. "You catch the first one? Fabulous. We're working with the lad, Frankie, getting him ready."

"Ready for what?" I asked. "The reconciliation?"

"I'm afraid not," said Madvig with a trace of sadness. "That's all over. *Fini.* We're just going through the motions until the final split. Di goes one way, the Prince goes another. What we're getting him ready for is life in Splitsville. A complete image overhaul. Take the starch out, make him a pop celebrity. Any ideas for a slogan? You were always good on slogans, Frankie. Vandercleve: A Mensch for the Times. Fortune bagels, wasn't it? Brilliant. What's that?"

"What's what?"

"That phallic thing there, middle of the green."

"The Washington Monument," I replied, somewhat shaken. Jet lag, I hoped, because if he wasn't the answer to my problems, nobody was.

He reached into his tweed jacket, produced a pair of Christian Dior granny specs, and slipped them on. "By God, you're right," he said. "Vanity, Frankie, vanity. Can't see a damned thing without these anymore, but hate to wear 'em. Ah, yes, the Monument. And there's the White House—which brings us to what you've been up to, Frankie. Your phone call was rather cryptic."

"It's a long story," I said, as we traveled down 15th Street toward the hotel. "Let's wait till you're settled in."

★ 176 ★

"Well, something's amiss, I've known that for weeks," he said.

"Oh? How so?"

"Never known a Vice President to get that much ink," replied my old mentor, still the Silver Fox of yore. "Knowing you, I told myself one of two things has happened: Bully's either bonkers or he's dead."

*Transcript, Tape No. 399-T, conversation between Frank Lee, press secretary to the Vice President, and Phil Madvig, public relations counsel to the House of Windsor, 7 June (1230 hours).*

PM: Well, you've created a monster, my boy, a monster, but all's well if we learn something from it.

FL: I doubt, really, I'll ever have this exact set of circumstances. . . .

PM: Don't mean that, of course. No two accounts are ever alike. Last time anything like this came up it was an eccentric billionaire. Remember dear old Howard? Dead five years before we got around to announcing it.

FL: That's right, you did handle that—

PM: Then there was Franco, of course. Picked that account up eight weeks after he died and kept him alive a year after that—until they'd arranged a decent succession. But then, the Spanish, they look at it quite differently from the way we do. Corruption empowers, they say, absolute corruption empowers absolutely. Or used to say. Haven't handled anything there in eons. But back to your dilemma. You really don't comprehend how it got out of hand?

FL: Frankly, no. I can't figure it. All I wanted was to get enough going—gaffes, controversy—to keep up appearances, cover Bully's absence. Then one thing—

PM: Led to two others. That's how it goes when a PR project gets rolling, Frankie. You are, as you've surmised, the victim of your own success. You started with a live Vice President about to be dumped, end up with a dead one about to be drafted for President.

FL: If he isn't indicted, cited, or impeached. Not to mention the vote in the Senate. No phone-ins there. We need a live—you think of something? I recognize the look.

PM: What you just said about phone-ins. Go over that story you told about what's-his-voice again?

FL: Feinbaum? The cover story? I told him, let's see—the KGB had tapped into the White House, the Vice President was on a secret overseas mission, and the President needed—

PM: Secret overseas mission.

FL: What?

PM: You don't need me, Frankie. I'm headed back to London. You've had the answer all along.

FL: Answer?

PM: It's right there, in your cover story to what's-his-voice.

FL: You're traveling too fast for me, chief. . . .

PM: The Vice President, Frankie—he can't talk to Stanton's committee, can't preside over the Senate, won't be around when Castro comes to Washington, because—you tell me Frankie.

FL: He's on a secret mission overseas!

PM: Good show. Brilliant, Frankie, brilliant. Just like the bagels.


Strong signed off on the idea before I even got to the part about how we'd leak word of the "mission" to the press. Ditto Cissy Vandercleve (reached between speaking engagements in the Far and Middle West). The President—told it was all a cover-up for

Bully's being shipped to a Texas sanitarium for a rest cure—had his first good night's sleep in a week.

The spin, of course, was that the "secret" overseas mission wouldn't be secret but a matter of front-page speculation. That Madvig figured, would get the Stanton Committee off the Vice President's back and explain why he wasn't around for any tie votes or summit events.

But how to leak the secret? One possibility was to patch things up with Ben Colfax by giving him a "high government source" exclusive. But since my credibility with Colfax was at an all-time low, there was always the chance that he'd debunk the story before it even floated.

The solution was to take Otto De Faye up on his offer of a hairstyling.

*Excerpt of transcript, Tape No. 429-A, conversation between Frank Lee, press secretary to the Vice President, Otto De Faye, "The Hairstylist of Presidents," 13 June (1730 hours).*

FL:     No, really, I'm not the type. . . .

OD:    Of course you are. Is it your age, is that it? Just last week I gave one to a seventy-year-old Supreme Court Justice and he walked out feeling thirty years younger. You know Justice Funk? Marvelous man. He was telling me about a case he's working on—he relaxes, feels he can let his hair down here.

FL:     Justice Funk got a friz?

OD:    Certainly. It was his wife's idea. He's remarried, you know. Lovely girl. Thirty, thirty-one years old. I used to style her first husband. Poor chap. Drank himself—

FL:     No time for a friz, Otto. Has the salon cleared out?

OD:    You're the last client of the day. When she made the appointment, your assistant—Ms. Braunschweig?—she said you wanted to discuss a confidential matter concerning my friend, the Vice President.

FL:     Confidential until now, Otto. Remember what the President wrote you about the Vice President's being involved—

OD:     In a matter involving national security. Yes, and I haven't breathed a word. If anything's out, it wasn't—

FL:     Of course not. But now, Otto, the signals have been switched. We want the word out, except it can't come from an official source, you know. We need someone we can trust—a person with contacts, who knows the right people—to get the word out. You sure the place is empty?

OD:     Positive.

FL:     Otto, my boss—your friend, the Vice President—is at this very moment . . .

FYI, the reason I didn't use Romie Clay as my leakee is that she'd have demanded an exclusive. What I needed was a wholesale, not a retail outlet. But to keep Romie happy I came up with an exclusive angle she could use—that the Vice President's secret mission was "closely tied" to the upcoming summit with Castro.

My mistake, but by that time who was counting?

De Faye's first appointment the next morning was the British ambassador, which explains why the story broke in London, high-tea time, about noon in Washington:

BBC'S WASHINGTON BUREAU HAS LEARNED THAT THE WHITE HOUSE HAS DISPATCHED VICE PRESIDENT STEWART VANDER-CLEVE ON AN OVERSEAS MISSION TO PARTS UNKNOWN. WHILE OFFICIAL SOURCES IN THE AMERICAN CAPITAL REFUSE COMMENT ON THE VICE PRESIDENT'S WHEREABOUTS, RUMORS ARE CIRCULATING IN SEVERAL FOREIGN CAPITALS—BONN, ANKARA, AND RIYADH—THAT A PLANE WITH U.S. STATE DEPARTMENT MARKINGS HAS TOUCHED DOWN WITHIN THE PAST TWENTY-FOUR HOURS . . .

Oh, yes, the State Department. The Secretary threw a tantrum. *Why hadn't he been advised? What was Vandercleve up to?* Strong told him to stick to foreign policy and leave the secret missions to the White House.

All four news networks, the wire services, both editions of the *Post* (Washington and New York), the three editions of the *Times* (Washington, New York, L.A.), *Baltimore Sun, Boston Globe,* and *Chicago Trib* went front page with the story on Day Two.

*Washington Post* headline:

### WHITE HOUSE ANGRY OVER
### VANDERCLEVE MISSION LEAK
#### "OUTRAGE" SAYS TOP STAFFER

Madvig's idea. A leak without official outrage would look suspicious, he pointed out. Strong played his part perfectly—in fact, outdid himself. He made everybody on the White House staff (including Mrs. Kaltenborn) take lie-detector tests.

By Day Two Bully had been spotted on five continents (including Antarctica, by a snow-blind Russian observer). His presence in the city was uncategorically denied in seven foreign capitals, categorically denied in two. A London tabloid and a Paris magazine ran almost identical stories (both written by the same free lance) that featured an eye-witness account by a plane mechanic who claimed he'd seen the American Vice President talking to "someone who looked like the Prime Minister [in Paris, the President of the Republic] in a secluded hanger at Heathrow/Charles DeGaulle airport."

By Day Three, the mission was credible enough to be second-guessed.

*The New York Times* headline:

## VANDERCLEVE MISSION VIEWED
## AS DIPLOMATIC BLUNDER

Coverage on Day Four led off with a nice four-color front-page map in *USA Today,* pinpointing the sixteen cities on seven continents where the Vice President had been spotted in the past forty-eight hours, all under the headline, ANYBODY HERE SEEN BULLY?

By Day Five, the gossip columns had caught up with the story, two items—one in the *New York Daily News,* the other in the *San Francisco Examiner*—reporting that the Vice President had left Washington for personal, not diplomatic, reasons: He and the Second Lady weren't speaking because of *her* recent travels.

Asked about the rumor at a Denver airport—she'd just made a speech there and was headed to Dallas for another—Cissy Vandercleve dismissed it, telling the reporter, quote, *Our marriage has never been more tranquil,* unquote.

The TV talk shows took over Days Six through Nine, with Henry Kissinger—remembered for his secret mission to China in the early seventies—back in vogue as a guest on "Today," "Good Morning, America," "Meet the Press," and "Face the Nation." Then there was *"Hoolihan's Free-for-All,"* a Washington discussion group that included, along with Host James Hoolihan, Columnist Mike Farley, Reporter Roberta Levine, and my old friend Ben Colfax.

*Excerpt, "Hoolihan's Free-for-All," syndicated television talk show (taped 6/16):*

HOOLIHAN:  Item One! The Vice President takes a powder. On the virtual eve of Fidel Castro's visit to Washington, Vice President Bully Vandercleve has gone off the screen—dispatched by the White House on an overseas mission, for reasons unknown. Opinions on the why and wherefore of the Vice President's journey abound, but what say you, Ben Colfax?

COLFAX: Hoolihan, if you had the good sense God gave little green apples, you'd know that this is the most over-rated political story of the year. It's perfectly appar-ent what the White House and Vandercleve are up to—

HOOLIHAN: Which is?

COLFAX: Stop interrupting.

HOOLIHAN: I wasn't interrupting, merely—

FARLEY: What makes you think the story's overrated? When a Vice President is handed a foreign policy assign-ment four weeks before the Republican conven-tion—

COLFAX: Farley, what you know about Republican conven-tions I could put into a thimble and—

HOOLIHAN: Of course, there are those who say the Vice Presi-dent is only too happy to be out of the country right now, because of the Stanton investigation.

LEVINE: The Stanton investigation is petty, partisan politics— Democratic sniping at its worst.

HOOLIHAN: But Stanton is a Republican—

FARLEY: In name only. I happen to agree with Roberta, Stan-ton's playing right into the Democrats' hands for the fall election. No, if you ask me, the reason Vander-cleve's left the country is to protest the Castro sum-mit—

COLFAX: Hey, wait a min—

LEVINE: And I agree with Mike. The feeling among people on the Hill I've talked to is that Vandercleve is very much against Castro's coming and—

★ 183 ★

HOOLIHAN: You agree with Mike? Mike agrees with you? Somebody agrees with somebody? A first—

COLFAX: I said—Hey, wait a minute! Is anybody interested in my opinion? The question, remember, was directed to me—and in my view—

HOOLIHAN: Item Two! After this commercial message . . .

A week before the Castro visit, Bully did the hat trick—the first time ever, not only in his career but in the history of the Vice Presidency.

Three cover stories:

First, *Newsweek.*

Second, *U.S. News & World Report.*

Third, *Time,* with the cover caption, "Vandercleve: Man on a Mission." If only he could have been there to see it. . . .

**BULLY COME HOME!**
*Your Country Needs You*
—*Placard seen at Anti-Castro rally,*
*Washington Monument grounds, June 20*

# BLAIR HOUSE
## JUNE 20 (5:15 P.M.)

"El primer punto de nuestra agenda es la pregunta, ¿Dónde está el Vice Presidente?"

*The first item on our agenda is the question, where is the Vice President?*

"Cuando el Presidente no me dice dónde está su Vice Presidente, nuestra única conclusión puede ser que los Estados Unidos está otra vez envuelto en un complot para derribar a mi gobierno."

*When the President won't tell me where the Vice President is, our only conclusion can be that the United States is again involved in a plot to overthrow my government.*

Castro saw the beads of sweat on El Presidente's forehead, the sick smile on his face as the words were translated. It confirmed what he'd suspected—what the woman reporter (whose name he couldn't remember) had learned from a White House source: That Vandercleve's trip was tied to the summit.

Summit! What a fraud! A trick, nothing more—*malas mañas capitalistas.* Castro hadn't liked the idea from the start, but that *idiota* in the Kremlin had pushed him into it. Now he was expected to stay in Washington the better part of a week, while Vandercleve was overseas on his *misión secreta,* stirring up trouble for Cuba.

Castro had other ideas, however. He was in Washington, but not for long. There'd been too many calculated snubs. First, the strings the *norteamericanos* had put on that invitation to address a joint session of Congress. A forty-five-minute time limit on a speech? *¡Ridículo!*

He'd hardly get through his acknowledgments in forty-five minutes. And those *burgueses* demonstrators lining the streets as he came into town? Who arranged *them?* His hosts, *los cerdos imperialistas!* And telling his Cuban delegation that the President's wife, *la Primera Señora,* preferred *no fumar* at the White House social functions, a clear provocation. . . .

Enough. By this time tomorrow, he'd be back in Havana. But not without leaving the treacherous *gringos* a scene to remember.

*Transcript, Tape No. 349-A, translated conversation between Fidel Castro and unidentified aide, Blair House, 20 June (1745 hours).*

UNIDENTIFIED AIDE:    Fidel!

FC:                              What's going on?

| UA: | Listen! We have information that the Vice President isn't on a secret mission! He's dead! |
| FC: | Dead! Who says so? |
| UA: | A gardener at the Vice President's residence—he's one of our agents—says the man hasn't been seen in five weeks. |
| FC: | A gardener? Fire him! He's a double agent passing on disinformation from the CIA. |

*From the* Washington Post *"Style" section, excerpt of list of invitees to White House dinner for Cuban Premier Fidel Castro, June 20*

Senator Herschel Klopfelter and wife, Amy
Ambassador Raphael Lavalier of France and friend,
    Justine Barras
Mr. Frank Lee, wife Maureen, and son Thomas . . .

# THE WHITE HOUSE

JUNE 20 (7:00 P.M.)

It was a first. Mo, who had always kept her McGovernite distance from a Republican White House, had agreed to attend the Castro dinner—the hottest social ticket in Washington since Michael Jackson played the East Room in the late eighties—after I'd wangled an invitation for Tommy.

True, as a Yuppie-generation suburban conformist, I hardly approved his precocious taste for far-Left heroes (a life-size blowup of Che Guevara in his bedroom, where normal American boys have poster art from *The Texas Chain Saw Massacre Part XI*). But after our little commencement misunderstanding, I owed him one. And Strong certainly owed me several hot tickets after I'd subjected myself, beyond the call, to Otto De Faye's barbarous shears. It would, however, grow out, Mo reassured me, even as Operation Avis (ten days, twelve hours left) would pass into limbo.

In a shimmering gray Donna Karan gown, she looked resplendent (to my biased eyes), as we moved up the receiving line toward the President who, reminded by an aide that I was the Vice President's press secretary, passed me on to the First Lady who, with passionate insincerity, expressed regret that the Vice President and "dear Cissy" couldn't be with us on this night of nights, then introduced us to the premier attraction of the hour.

Behind Fidel, whose beard had turned pure salt since I'd last seen him (Romie Clay's interview several years before), a protocol aide leaned over to repeat our names, then added *(sotto voce)*, *"El trabaja para Vandercleve"*; at which instant Castro glowered, stiffened, and looked past us, down the line.

Snubbed; but onward. . . .

At the pre-prandial reception in the East Room, my quick head count (a hustler's skill keened during Bully's campaigns) came to 118, give or take a Senator, film star, campaign contributor, or Castro minion. The chief topics for the evening being the historic nature of the occasion and the whereabouts of my employer, I welcomed the early advent of a cadre of White House ushers, signaling that soup was on, since—my identity having been broadcast by a garrulous fat-cat—I'd begun to draw an unruly crowd.

Once in the State Dining Room we were welcomed by a string quartet (clearly on remainder from a recent visit by the Israeli prime minister) playing a medley from *Fiddler on the Roof.* U.S. and Cuban flags flanked a room filled with ten circular tables, each centered by an epergne containing red, white, and sprayed-blue roses. Mo sat at Table 8, between a mufti-clad Cuban minister and a senior member of the House Foreign Affairs Committee, an off-the-wall Democrat sure to keep the conversation rolling, whether or not their Cuban tablemates spoke or acknowledged English during the course of the evening.

Ah, yes, Castro's dictum regarding the bilingual nature of the summit: One hour before guests were due to arrive at the White House, U.S. Protocol was put on notice that the Cuban delegation would neither speak nor acknowledge any language but their own at this or any other summit session. Informed that the rule posed certain problems—no arrangements had been made for that many interpreters—Castro's emissary (according to reports in the next day's papers) appeared rather pleased, hastening back to Blair House to pass the good word. There followed some hasty reshuffling to provide at least one Spanish-speaking *Yanqui* per table, an improv that seemed to work things out—save at Table 10, where the designated interpreter's credentials were summarily challenged by the Cuban Minister of Education, who rudely asserted that in *her* country, *jóvenes de pocos años* were preparing for bed at that hour.

At another time or place I would have expected Tommy to reply with an annotated disquisition on bourgeois conformist mindsets regarding societal discipline. Instead, like any good interpreter, he passed the comment along to the party who could best answer it.

I explained to the Minister that ordinarily sixteen-year-olds didn't attend White House dinners, but in our interpreter's case an exception had been made because of his exemplary performance in school. She was unimpressed; that was the only interpretation I could make of her uncivil response, which was to pluck my name card off the table, examine it, then ask, *"¿Quién es?"*

*"El es mi padre,"* began my interpreter, thinking to save time. Then, before I could stop him—for I had a professional premonition, you see, of yet another PR disaster in the making—he had said it. *"El trabaja para el Vice Presidente."*

And it was done. *Terminado.*

*"¿El Vice Presidente? ¿Dónde está?"*

Table 10, of course, was only a microcosm of the total disaster that would befall the First Lady's night of nights, for the question that consumed us—rack of lamb through lemon souffle—would be asked by various counts (there was no transcript) no fewer than forty-seven times by Fidel Castro during his two-hour, fifty-minute response to the President's ceremonial toast to peace and understanding.

The trap—Fidel's *Emboscada*—was sprung at 9:37 P.M., seven minutes after the networks, at White House urging, had cut into their regular programming to carry the President's toast. When the President finished, Castro, who was seated next to the First Lady, rose, raised his glass, unceremoniously drained it, then looking at the First Lady, remarked that although he hadn't indulged in years, this seemed an appropriate moment to reacquaint himself with the *gusto* of good Cuban tobacco.

In Spanish, of course, though the act itself—the moral equivalent of war—needed no translation.

Not in three and a half years had anyone—not the President, not the King of Spain, not even the firebrand Senator from North Carolina—defied the First Lady's injunction against the use of tobacco at White House social functions. But now, on signal, the entire Cuban delegation to the summit (including the Minister of Education) was lighting up. Smoke curled and billowed across the State Dining Room.

Then Fidel began to speak.

By 10:00 P.M., allowing time for translation, the history of U.S.–Cuban relations leading up to the Revolution had been covered. The first of the networks began cutting away.

By 10:30, U.S.–Cuban relations leading up to the Bay of Pigs had been covered. The last of the networks cut away.

By 11:00 P.M., U.S.–Cuban relations through the Johnson-Nixon years had been covered. Fidel paused, examined the dead ash of his *cigarro,* dropped it into his fingerbowl, and lit another. Tables 5, 7, and 9 began cutting away.

By 11:30 P.M., U.S.–Cuban relations through the *imperialista* Reagan years had been covered. The First Lady, who a half hour before had considered feigning illness, was now genuinely ill. She cut away.

By midnight, U.S.–Cuban relations up to the advent of the current administration had been covered. Fidel opened his jacket and turned toward the President. *"¿Dónde?"* he demanded. *"¿El Vice Presidente? ¿Dónde está?"*

He would, in the course of denouncing *Yanqui* treachery, repeat the question forty-six times in the next twenty-seven minutes; then grind out his *cigarro,* declare the summit *acabado, terminado, torpeado,* and leave the White House, headed back to Havana.

Out of the 120 who were present and accounted for at the beginning of the night of nights, there were, excluding the president, only seven of us there at the end to see history in the making.

### ADIÓS, GRINGO!
### FIDEL STORMS OUT
### OF CASA BLANCA

*—Front page,*
New York Daily News,
*final edition, June 21*

### FIDEL CASTRO DENOUNCES U.S.
### IN FIERY WALKOUT
#### SUDDEN COLLAPSE OF SUMMIT
#### SHAKES WHITE HOUSE

*—Banner, front-page headline,*
The New York Times, *June 21*

### DEMOCRATS SEE CASTRO REBUFF AS
### MAJOR ISSUE IN FALL CAMPAIGN

*—Headline, page 1,*
Washington Post, *June 22*

Headline and excerpt, the Bottoms-Colfax column, *Washington Post,* June 24:

## Vandercleve's Mission:
## The Inside Story

The Vice President's "secret mission"—real or cover-up?

As readers know, the authors of this column took a skeptical view of the Vandercleve "mission" from the day the story broke—or more accurately, was leaked—at the White House. Now, with the inside story revealed by a source close to the Vice President, our suspicions have been confirmed.

Fact: Bully Vandercleve was indeed absent from the country the day his "secret mission" story broke in London—but not to carry out some clandestine diplomatic assignment on behalf of the President. On the contrary, Vandercleve left Washington for an "extended" overseas trip because he had serious misgivings about the President's plans to reach an election-year peace accord with Cuba's Castro regime.

"The Vice President just didn't want to be around when the summit took place," our source informed us. "He felt having Castro come to Washington was a serious mistake and it turned out he was right. . . ."

*". . . it turned out he was right."*

Just the single most important line to come out of Operation Avis; and FYI, for all my skill in not only keeping Vice President Stewart B. Vandercleve in the public eye but damned near getting him renominated *six weeks after he died*—for all that, *I* wasn't the PR genius who planted it.

It was McCluskey, of all people. Give him the credit. Here's how, as Maximilian Mize would say, it eventuated:

Ben Colfax was still in heat to uncover the "truth" about Bully's inaccessibility for interviews. *Did it have anything to do with the Castro summit?* Replaying the tape of Feinbaum's late-night insult session with Joe Bristle, he came to Bully's line about hiding the silverware if Fidel ever dined at the White House. Thin

★ **191** ★

stuff, but it was a slow news day and Colfax wanted a fresh angle on the summit collapse. Vandercleve being dumped was stale copy. Vandercleve dumping on others—Castro, and by implication the man who invited him to dine at the White House—that had possibilities. Not that Colfax was trying to do the Vice President any favors. But an angle was an angle.

He didn't call the press office, of course. I'd tried to sucker him with that dumb line about Bully's being dead, and he knew Carla wouldn't talk without first checking with me. So Colfax came up with one of the oldest plays out of the White House press book: an end run, around the press secretary to the chief of staff. . . .

*Transcript, Tape No. 258-X, excerpt of telephone conversation between Martin McCluskey, Vice President's chief of staff, and Ben Colfax, syndicated columnist, 23 June (1025 hours).*

MM: Mr. Colfax, I'm afraid there's been some mistake. You want the press off—

BC: No mistake. I've got a lead on a story that the Vice President had some reservations about the Castro visit. Can you tell me anything about that?

MM: You want to talk to Frank Lee. He's the—

BC: Is this Extension 4213?

MM: Yes.

BC: You're Martin McCluskey, the Vice President's chief of staff?

MM: Yes.

BC: Does the title mean anything or is it just one more piece of *(expletive deleted)* handed out by the Vice President's office? You make how much? Sixty-seven thou a year? Public money?

MM: Yes, but—

BC: Then why can't I, representing the public, get a straight answer from you, a public servant? I'll ask again: Did Vice President Vandercleve have any reservations about Fidel Castro's visit?

MM: Reservations?

BC: You see, Marty—is it Marty?

MM: Friends call me Mac.

BC: You see, Mac, the way I read this situation, having Castro to the White House was such an incredibly stupid idea that I've got to believe at least one person in the administration had brains enough to try to deep-six it.

MM: Well, since you put it that way, I'm sure the Vice President would have expressed some reservations.

BC: Serious reservations? After all, it was a serious *(expletive deleted)*-up.

MM: Yes, he would have had serious reservations, I'm sure.

BC: And that secret mission—

MM: I won't go into anything about the secret mission.

BC: I wouldn't expect you to. But we can assume that if the Vice President had serious reservations, he wouldn't want to be around when Castro came to town, right?

MM: Yes, I'd say so.

BC: I mean, the Vice President did think it was a serious mistake.

MM: Well, considering Castro's outrageous performance, yes, it certainly was a serious—

BC: But your office has nothing to be ashamed of. After all, it turned out your boss was right all along.

MM: Pardon?

BC: The Vice President was right.

MM: Yes, of course, always.

BC: Yeah, well, thanks, Mac, for your time. We got started on the wrong foot but—

MM: You do understand, don't you, why I'm not the one to talk to? I wish I could be more helpful, but—

BC: Understood. Oh, one last thing. Everything you did say is on the record, right?

MM: On the record?

BC: Of course, I won't quote you directly, but there's nothing you said about how the Vice President felt that you wouldn't want the American public to know, is there?

MM: Of course not—though I really, you know, didn't say all that much. . . .

## THE WHITE HOUSE WEST WING

### JUNE 26 (8:15 A.M.)

Back on the palmière list, with a flourish. The difference this time was that Strong sent a chauffeur to pick me up who drove as if it mattered that I arrive in one piece.

We rolled past the southwest gate a little after seven, windshield wipers flailing against a spring downpour. A Marine guard met me at the West Executive entrance with an umbrella, and I was hardly past the threshold of Strong's office when Mrs. Kaltenborn filled my hands with morning treats.

"Cute trick," said Strong after Mrs. K. left us alone. He reached across his desk to hand me a batch of clippings. "Columns, interpretive pieces, editorials that all appeared in the past forty-eight hours," he explained. "Your boss is a frigging hero of the Republic, Lee. A man of principle who leaves the country rather than butter up a dirty Commie. The lone voice of sanity who saw what was coming. Very cute trick—though where the hell it gets you is beyond me."

I set down my cup and riffled through the clips. From the *Boston Globe:*

## VANDERCLEVE SAID TO BE IN SPAIN
### IN SECLUSION AT REMOTE FAMILY VILLA

From the *San Diego Tribune:*

## BULLY WITH FRIENDS ON SOUTH PACIFIC ISLE
### 'MISSION' STORY NOW DOUBTED

"Take a look at the Stanton interview," said Strong. "You think that sonofabitch doesn't follow the polls?"

From the *Wall Street Journal:*

## STANTON COMMITTEE RECESSES FOR SUMMER
### SENATOR TERMS RUMORS OF V.P. SUBPOENA "BASELESS"

"Cute trick," Strong repeated. He strode across the room to straighten a wall portrait of C. Bascom Slemp, Calvin Coolidge's chief of staff.

"Why do you keep saying, 'cute trick'?" I asked. "It's not as if anybody actually *planned* this coverage. McCluskey sourced it, then the thing took legs on its own. You know how that happens."

"What I know," replied Strong, studying the portrait and shaking his head side to side, "is that the President of the United States is up at Camp David looking at delegate counts that say the nomination could go either way. And reading public opinion surveys

★ **195** ★

that show the summit brought his numbers down twenty points and his batty Vice President's up twenty-five. How does that look?"

"From where the President sits, none too good," I replied.

"I mean the frame," replied Strong, studying the portrait with narrowed eyes, an elbow perched on a cupped hand. "Can't tell from here."

"A trifle higher on the right," I said.

He adjusted the frame, stepped back, and looked my way. I nodded, affirmative.

"Good," he said, returning to his desk chair. "Crooked frames drive me up the wall."

The intercom buzzed.

"Mr. Deutsch is here to drive you to the Pentagon pad," said Mrs. Kaltenborn. "The chopper's waiting."

"You're going somewhere?" I asked, returning a second pal-mière to the tray and rising to my feet.

*"We're* going somewhere," corrected Strong, stuffing papers into his briefcase. "Camp David. Why do you think you got the limo treatment? The President wants a preconvention showdown session, with somebody there representing your boss."

"The President wants me at Camp David to represent the Vice President?" I said. "I'm—I'm flattered."

"Don't be," replied Strong, headed toward the door. "It was down to you, McCluskey, or the wife."


*Transcript, Tape No. 371-Z group conference at Aspen Lodge, Camp David. Conferees: the President; Regis Strong, WH chief of staff; Frank Lee, press secretary to the Vice President; B. J. Crotty, CEO, Crotty Surveys, public opinion pollster, 26 June (1045 hours).*

RS:    Mr. President, this is Frank Lee, the Vice President's press secretary, and of course you know Crotty there. All right now, to bring everybody up to speed—

P:    Let's save time, Regis. If anybody's not up to speed, they don't belong here. I've been looking over these numbers, pre- and post-Castro. Horrendous dive. Changes the complexion of the race completely. My foreign policy performance numbers—a President's ace in the hole—awful. If I could get my hands on that Brillo-faced Communist *(expletive deleted)*, I'd *(inaudible)*.

RS:   Mr. President, settle down. The last thing we need is—you want a glass of water, sir?

P:    No, let's get on with it. I've had time to think in the last few days, and I've reached certain conclusions. Crotty?

BJC:  Yes, sir?

P:    Crotty, how do your numbers look for November? Me against the most likely Democrat. Kennedy? Roosevelt?

BJC:  Well, sir, that depends on what Kennedy or Roosevelt wins their nomination. The options there—

P:    Specifically—if foreign policy becomes the Number One issue, which Kennedy or Roosevelt—I assume this Masked Marvel candidate, he's not going anywhere, right?

BJC:  No, sir, he's strictly a gimmick candidate, not going anywhere. But if I understand your question, yes, foreign policy has definitely moved to the front burner as an issue—no matter which Democrat you run against.

P:    Right. Now we've got this situation—Stanton isn't my long-range problem. Not that there isn't a chance the *(expletive deleted)* won't wax me at the convention. That ball's in the air. But in our position, we have to look ahead. The nomination's not worth a bucket of warm *(expletive deleted)* unless you've got the tools to win in November. You follow, Regis?

RS:   I follow. We've got to come out of the convention geared for a general—

P:  A general election where, according to Crotty's numbers, foreign not domestic policy will be the big issue. Is that right, Crotty?

BJC:  A big issue, sir.

P:  Right. And that means our whole strategy on this Vice Presidential thing has got to change.

RS:  Change?

P:  Hear me out, Regis. I've given a lot of thought to this, and my conclusion is that none of these governors we've promised the Vice Presidency to—how many are there now, Regis?

RS:  I'll check the latest total, sir.

P:  Just give me a rough count.

RS:  Oh, ten, eleven, with three more on the fence we plan to talk to, the next few days—

P:  No need. Not one of them—no governor—can help me where I'm bleeding worst.

RS:  I don't follow, sir.

P:  The Castro thing. I need somebody on the ticket who can cover me there. According to the numbers, there's only one, whether I like the prospect or not. Just one.

RS:  Sir?

P:  Have you checked Vandercleve's numbers on that front, Regis? You know, I told you that *(expletive deleted)* was up to something. Crazy or not—oh, Lee, forgot you were here—ah—How's the Vice President coming along? Will he be out of the—uh—hospital anytime soon? Back on his feet?

FL:  Oh, yes, sir. Out any day.

P:  Well, that's good to know, Fred—and this is why I wanted you here today.

RS: Frank.

P: Yes, Frank, of course. Why I wanted you here. Conditions have changed in the past six weeks—especially the past week. As I looked at the numbers last night and this morning, it's perfectly clear only one man can help me where I need help, not only at the convention next week but in the general.

RS: Sir, are you suggesting what I think?

P: Vandercleve, Regis, Vandercleve—whether we like it or not. Excuse, Lee, excuse my candor, but you know, Bully and I haven't always seen—

FL: Yes, sir.

RS: No, sir. That—that just won't work at all. With due respect—

P: Why won't it work? Because Vandercleve's been under a— uh—nervous strain lately? The way I tracked his numbers, he's never done better politically. If he'd run against me four years ago like he's campaigned to keep from being dumped the last six weeks, he'd be President, not me.

RS: It's just not that simple, sir. Vandercleve is a loose cannon—

P: Because he's down in Texas, convalescing? We know that, everybody in this room knows that, but—

BJC: I didn't know that. I thought he was on some kind of overseas mission. Either that or off somewhere in a sulk because of Castro's being invited.

P: There, you see, Regis? Crotty there's as sophisticated a voter as you can find, and he didn't know Vandercleve's convalescing in a Texas hospital.

BJC: I sure as *(expletive deleted)* didn't.

P: That's because Lee there has done such a *(expletive deleted)* good job. Now the way I see it, Regis, Lee just keeps right on doing the job. We bring the Vice President out of the

★ 199 ★

hospital in time for the convention, settle him down—I'd look to you for help on that front, Fred—

FL: Frank.

P: Frank. You and, I assume, Mrs. Vandercleve could help keep him settled for the duration of the campaign. Schedule him carefully, watch his mood swings.

RS: Mr. President, it just won't—

P: Won't what, Regis? Look, I know how deeply you're committed to the original plan. *(Expletive deleted),* I was, too. But a governor—half a dozen governors—won't put me over the top in November. Beating Stanton for the nomination won't be—

RS: Mr. President, believe me—have I ever steered you wrong, sir?

P: What's that got to do with it? Look, Regis, you seem to forget at times that I'm—I'm—the one who makes the final decisions around here. And I've made up my mind, *(expletive deleted)* it. We announce the first day of the convention that Bully Vandercleve stays on the ticket as my Vice President. Period. No further discussion.

RS: Tell him, Lee.

P: Tell me what?

RS: Sir, we had wanted to spare you— Go ahead, Lee, tell him. He won't believe me. Tell him why your boss won't show up at the convention for an acceptance speech even if he's back on the ticket.

FL: You mean, because he's on a secret mission? That he's—

RS: No, I mean tell him the real *(expletive deleted)* truth, the whole *(expletive deleted)* story.

P: What story? Tell me what story? What have you been up to, Regis? What are you holding out on me this time? The Vice

President's bonkers, right? Crazy. Okay, we'll just have to live with it.

RS: That's not it, Mr. President. If that's all there was—

P: There's more? Something worse? What? What's worse? Tell me, Lee, tell me! As your President, as Commander-in-Chief, as Leader of the Free World, I direct you to—

FL: Sir, the Vice President is dead.

P: Was dead, yes. But political situations change, Lee, and your boss's fortunes have revived. In fact, he's more of an asset now, after the Castro thing, than he was four years ago when—

FL: No, sir. I mean the Vice President is dead. He's no longer with us. Passed on. He's been dead for six weeks.

P: Dead? Dead for six weeks? But I talked to him—

FL: No, sir. You talked to Moishe Feinbaum. The Vice President is—

P: Feinbaum? Not Vandercleve? Vandercleve's dead? Couldn't campaign if nominated? Couldn't be sworn in if elected? Dead? That *(expletive deleted)*, it's typical—He'd do anything—absolutely anything—

RS: Mr. President! Look out, sir! Somebody catch—

FL: Mr. President!

BJC: My God, is he . . . ?

RS: Get the agent outside the door, tell him to get the Doc. Lousy luck, Lee, I mean lousy luck. Two days before the *(expletive deleted)* convention, only two days. What a *(expletive deleted)*-poor time he takes to pull something like this.

# 9

SENATOR HEFFERNAN:    Will the witness state his name? I repeat, will the witness state his name? Let the record show that the witness is Kurt Deutsch, who served as special assistant to White House Chief of Staff Regis Strong. Mr. Deutsch, I am going to ask you a series of questions regarding the subject of this investigation—reading from the Committee's charter—"the willful and deliberate withholding of information regarding the death of Vice President Stewart Bulloch Vandercleve, by means of a vast conspiracy designed to alter the outcome of the Republican party's presidential nominating process."

SENATOR MORGAN:    If the Chairman will yield?

SENATOR HEFFERNAN:    Yes, certainly.

SENATOR MORGAN:    Let me point out to the witness that this Committee has already obtained considerable testimony from more than three dozen persons involved in the Vandercleve Succession Conspiracy, and his unwillingness to cooperate will serve no purpose other than to prejudice his own case, not only in the courts but in the eyes of the American people.

SENATOR HEFFERNAN:    I concur in the remarks of the gentleman from Kentucky. Again I ask, will the witness please state his name? All right, let me try another approach: Is it the witness's purpose to claim immunity from testifying under the Fifth Amendment to the U.S. Constitution? Let the record show the witness refuses to answer. Under the First Amendment? Let the record show the witness refuses to answer. Under the Tenth Amendment? Let the record show . . .

# ★ FYI ★

★ Let my record show that when the time came, I not only appeared before the Committee voluntarily, but was commended at the end of my testimony (five full days, all four networks) for an "honest, forthright recital" of my role in what *The Economist* first tagged "the Vandercleve Succession Conspiracy."

You can't please everybody, of course. Regis Strong—this was before his conversion—told me after I'd finished that my commendation and a buck-fifty would buy me a cup of Mrs. K.'s Special at her Power City Coffee & Pastry Shoppe near Pennsylvania and 17th, the hot new In spot for early-morning White House staffers.

Second only to Deutsch, Strong was the hardest-nosed of our Gang of Thirty-eight. Even after Doc Berger pronounced the President dead, RS had a big picture in mind for carrying the conspiracy to its—

RS: Logical conclusion. We've come this far, why back off now? The balloting for President starts in less than a week—

FL: Won't work, Strong. The Constitution's pretty clear on that point. Twenty-fifth Amendment. The President dies, the Vice President takes over—unless, of course, he's dead, in which case the people who knew he was dead and didn't tell anybody go to jail, directly to jail—

RS: You know, Lee, you had me fooled for a while. I actually thought you were coming up to speed on the big picture. Hear me out now. Your way, you know who becomes President? The *(expletive deleted)* Speaker of the House, not only an agrarian cretin from Iowa but a *(expletive deleted)* Democrat. My way, we keep this thing bottled for less than a week—the President doesn't have anything booked till the convention—then, the night before the balloting, I do a meeting with Stanton—

FL: To tell him the President and Vice President are dead? Ask him if he'll get on the Need to Know list? Somehow I don't think Stanton's the type—

RS: No, *(expletive deleted)*-hole, to do a deal with him. Tell him the President's pulling a Lyndon Johnson, stepping down rather than running the risk of getting his *(expletive deleted)* whipped. Make it sound like Hertz was talked into it by his inner circle—you're looking at it—so when Stanton gets nominated on the first ballot, he'll remember who his friends were. Then, twenty-four hours later, the President checks out with a stroke here at Camp David. Just like it happened, only tape delayed.

★ **206** ★

FL:   And the First Lady, the Secret Service, White House staff, President's family, friends . . . ?

RS:   I start work on them as soon as you're on board. You're all that's holding me up, Lee. Crotty's no problem. He's easy to handle. Just make sure he keeps his White House contract. But you, Lee, were the only other person in the room when it happened. And let's not forget the flip side.

FL:   Yeah?

RS:   Like what happens to your *(expletive deleted)* and mine if Operation Avis is blown. We're already in deep *(expletive deleted),* so what's the problem? We just upgrade Operation Avis to Operation Hertz-Avis for a week.

When Strong finished his pitch, I knew what my answer would be, but let me confess, for credibility's sake, that there was a moment of doubt when something my old mentor once said— about always having wanted his own President—came back to me. . . .

FL:   Give me some time, let me mull it over.

RS:   Take all the time you need. I'm headed down the hall, be back in ten minutes.

*Excerpt of transcript, Tape No. 356-R, transatlantic telephone conversation between Frank Lee, press secretary to the Vice President, and Philip Madvig, public relations adviser to the House of Windsor, 26 June (1200 hours).*

PM:   You didn't have to call, Frankie. You already know the answer. The Vice President's gone, now the President's gone. Rule Number One, remember? *What the client wants—*

FL:     *—the client gets.*

PM:     Exactly. Bully's had a great run, everything he could ask for. You got him back on the ticket, a Presidential boomlet, the cover of *Time.* What's left? Give the client what he wants, Frankie, what he wants. Let the poor *(expletive deleted)* die in peace. . . .

## Allenwood Federal Penitentiary
## "Prison of the Stars"
## Allenwood, Pennsylvania

April 10

Ms. Gwendolyn Dolittle
Amberson Hall
Newcomb College
7584 Willow Street
New Orleans, LA 50457

Dear Ms. Dolittle:

Received your interesting questionnaire regarding Operation Avis and only wish I could be of more help on your term paper. However, contractual commitments with a publisher prevent my answering all but your last question, "What's happened to the major players in Avis, along with others whose lives were touched by the Operation?"

According to legal counsel (my cellmate), the answer to that question contains information in the public domain, so in this particular case the publisher can go *(expletive deleted by prison censor)* himself. Here then is a breakdown on what's happened to major and minor figures involved in Operation Avis:

★   *C. Foster Abel.* Convicted on four counts of market manipulation, two of mishandling clients' funds. Sentenced to one year, now shares cell with another prominent Avis figure and is currently finishing book titled, *Playing the Big Board: Corporate Ethics in the Fast Lane.*

★   *Sam Andreas.* Retired from Secret Service without prejudice after Congressional investigators found that he and other members of the Service acted in good faith trying to protect the Vice President's reputation. Now chief of security for Kim-Chung Industries, worldwide manufacturer of surveillance devices headquartered in Seoul, Korea.

★   *Carla Braunschweig.* Also cleared by investigators for acting in good faith. Now press secretary to the Vice President of the United States.

★   *Romana Clay.* Resigned as TV network correspondent when Avis scandal broke. Later wrote best-selling book, *All the Vice President's Men,* soon to be released as motion picture starring Rob Lowe and Demi Moore. Frequently appears as guest host on David Letterman show.

★   *Ben Colfax.* Winner of the Pulitzer Prize in two categories for investigative reporting before and after Avis was exposed. Colfax's fictional treatment of the story, titled *Dirty Linen,* is being made into a television miniseries.

★   *Otto De Faye.* Still ranks as the National Capital's leading hairstylist. As a result of notoriety gained through his dupe's role in Avis, he now writes a monthly column, "Tonsorial Tips," for a major men's fashion magazine.

★ *Kurt Deutsch.* Sentenced to a total of 125 years for combination of offenses, including excessive surveillance, obstruction of justice, contempt of Congress (120 counts), unauthorized operation of an espionage safehouse, reckless driving (56 counts), and illegal cremation (1 count). Freed on technicality by appeals court after six months in prison, is suing government for restitution. Now a campus cult hero, Deutsch wrote best-selling life story, *Jugular,* currently being made into a TV miniseries. Touted by Hollywood agent as "the next Chuck Norris" in search-and-destroy genre films. Campus lecture fee: 10 Ks a pop, plus expenses and access to convenient practice range.

★ *Moishe Feinbaum.* Testified before Committee investigating Operation Avis for 5 days in 250 voices, including those of 25 out of 25 Committee members. Along with live-in wife Bubala (nee Helga) and gourmet chef *Nu?* (nee Nu), he was cleared of all charges. Wrote best-selling book based on his experience playing a dead Vice President. Title: *What Have You Done for Me Lately?*

★ *Lancelot Kaufman.* As Attorney General, rendered legal opinion justifying Operation Avis as "exigency of state." Cleared by Congressional committee, he retired from government service and now serves as adviser on constitutional law to several Latin American and Middle East cabinets.

★ *Maureen (Mo) Lee.* Cleared by Congressional committee. As wife of celebrated figure in Washington scandal, was asked to throw out first ball in Mets' Grapefruit League opener this year (Mets 4, Orioles 2). Now senior partner in law firm and more active than ever in Democratic party affairs. Also cleared: *Thomas S. Lee,* the couple's son who, after attending White House dinner for

Castro, swung Far Right, replacing life-sized bedroom poster of Che Guevara with one of Pat Buchanan.

★   *Philip Madvig.* Cleared. Still in London. Recently appointed Her Majesty's official Publicist Laureate.

★   *Martin McCluskey.* Cleared. Author of best-selling paperback, *Too Hot in the Kitchen,* a whistleblower's view of Operation Avis, now being made into a minor motion picture. Campus lecture fee: 1 K a pop, plus expenses and access to a convenient sanctuary.

★   *Max M. Mize.* Retired as FBI Director. Currently seeking funds to establish law-enforcement foundation. Recent author of *Circumventing Linguistic Caveats,* an instruction manual to help government agencies get their message through to the public.

★   *Royce Percival.* Reappointed, with raise, as headmaster of Barton Academy after Avis scandal broke and Cissy Vandercleve gave $10 million in her late husband's name to Academy's endowment fund.

★   *Berzelius (Buzz) Stanton.* Nominated Republican candidate for President on first ballot. Elected by narrow margin in November, along with running mate, the nation's first woman Vice President. Margin of victory: Hispanic vote in California and Southwest, where campaign rallies featured fortune enchiladas with message inside, *Stanton: Un Hombre Para Los Tiempos.*

★   *Regis Strong.* Found guilty on twenty-three counts of conspiring to abet the impersonation of a federal official and obstruction of justice. Sentenced to three years' imprisonment, eligible for parole in June. While in prison has undergone "profound religious conversion," leading him to write best-selling inspirational book, *God Was My*

*Co-conspirator.* Has contract with lecture bureau for series of campus appearances after release. Fee: 8 Ks a pop, plus expenses.

★    *Cissy Vandercleve.* Cleared by Committee after investigation found her "blameless" in Avis scandal, having been "misled" by White House and Vice President's aides. Took oath on Capitol steps as first woman Vice President in January.

Finally, Ms. Dolittle, we come to the major player *sans* whom (with due immodesty) there could have been no Operation Avis.

Having waived immunity (under advice of my lawyer/wife) I testified at length and was duly commended, celebrated (cover of *People*), and indicted on thirty-six counts of conspiring to abet, obstruction, forgery by Autopen, and a multitude of lesser crimes. Given a three-year sentence—one less, Bully would say, than a Vice President—I expect to be paroled June 1, thanks to exemplary behavior and an overcrowded prison system. My plans after that?

First, of course, an extended vacation *en famille,* a chance for Mo and me to tune out the discordant political notes of the past year, to recall the way the song used to go, words and music. Six cities in thirty days—New York, Atlanta, Philadelphia, Pittsburgh, St. Louis, Montreal. Not what you'd call the sun-and-sand capitals of the Western hemisphere, but you go where the band's playing and, unfortunately, the Mets aren't scheduled for St. Bart, the Bahamas, or La Jolla that early in the season.

Next, back to real life—life after Bully. When the ego goes, what's an alter to do?

As omens would have it, my future is made. Bids and offers, options and prospects, rainbows and gold, all the way. Unlike Regis Strong, I have undergone no religious conversion, profound or otherwise, since gaining status as a jailbird. But, like him, I have contracted with a speakers' bureau (The Gasser Group) that specializes in booking white-collar felons onto college campuses. There will be a nationwide tour in the fall—9 Ks a pop, expenses, and access to a Royal Standard Nonelectric to do my twice-a-week political column, "Frank Lee Speaking." And my book, of course, which promises—so my publisher says—to be not just big, but maybe the biggest ever in political confessionals.

We are talking, I mean, seven—even eight—figures in sales. Motion picture rights (Tommy sees my part being played by Richard Dreyfuss, though I've always thought of myself as more the Harrison Ford type.) And foreign rights. And TV rights. And sequels. And spin-offs. Nothing but blockbuster.

God, I wish Bully could be here to see it all happen. I always did tell him that if worse came to worst, I knew how to make it in the real world.

Sincerely,

*Frank Lee*

Frank Lee